BU...

UNIV...

C000185539

Enrico Tessarin

The summer of 1989

© 2022 **Europe Books**| London
www.europebooks.co.uk | info@europebooks.co.uk

ISBN 9791220121842
First edition: April 2022
Distribution for the United Kingdom: **Vine House
Distribution ltd**

Printed for Italy by Rotomail Italia
*Finito di stampare nel mese di giugno 2022
presso Rotomail Italia S.p.A. - Vignate (MI)*

The summer of 1989

Writing this book has been my dream since I was a child, but I would never have completed, let alone published it, without the love and support of Winnie Wong. Forever grateful.

Foreword

I wrote this book as I approached fifty years of age, determined to complete my first novel. I've always wanted to write a book, but I didn't know what to write about. Then one day, about five years ago, this idea struck me, and I started writing, frightened I would never finish and, even more, that what I was writing might not interest anyone. I very much enjoyed the process though, and the words have flowed easily.

Little by little I started to show my manuscript to people and, much to my delight, the feedback was good. Incredibly, the most favourable comments came from non-Italians who were totally unfamiliar with the story and the setting.

That gave me the will and energy to continue and to complete the book, which is a fictional reconstruction of what happened to me as an 18-year-old in the summer of '89. Most names have been changed, but the people who lived those years alongside me will recognise many others - some protagonists are still alive, some have died.

Writing this book has not been easy as it reveals a ghost that lay deep in my heart for many years. I never imagined it could be therapeutic, but I then found I needed closure. That period of my life is definitely over now.

And I am a father of two teenagers, so I feel more than ever that this book is important to me, if only as a reminder of what happened and its effect on my life.

Completing it has freed me and allowed me to brush away the past and start again - a new life.

Therefore, this book is dedicated to Winnie. Without you, your encouragement, and your patient love all the way to the last draft, this book would never have been completed.

Thank you, my rollercoaster love.

*Thank you to my children who are a source of con-
tinued inspiration. To my parents who tried to teach me
as much as possible even though I didn't quite listen,
and the friends from the Basta Sognare group.
One of the most wonderful constants in my life.
Grazie amici.*

"People think a soulmate is your perfect fit, and that's what everyone wants. But a true soulmate is a mirror, the person who shows you everything that is holding you back, the person who brings you to your own attention so you can change your life.

A true soulmate is probably the most important person you'll ever meet, because they tear down your walls and smack you awake. A soulmate's purpose is to shake you up, tear your ego apart a little bit, show you your obstacles and addictions, break your heart open so new light can get in, make you so desperate and out of control that you have to transform your life, then introduce you to your spiritual master "

Eat, pray, love
by Elizabeth Gilbert

Essential notes for the (non-Italian) reader:

A motorbike is essential for any Italian teenager, especially for one living in a small village with no public transport. Motorbikes are essential to move about, keep up with your friends and, most importantly, to pick up a girl from home. Specially in summer, when helmets were not compulsory and tank tops had just come onto the fashion scene.

In Italy any teenage girl will automatically judge a guy by his bike, so a small underpowered Piaggio Vespa means chances are that she won't stay your girlfriend for long. If you have an Aprilia Tuareg Rally then things will go much better.

No need to say the writer owned a Vespa and could only dream of a Tuareg Rally.

MAGGIORATA (oversize) = Typical Italian stereotype of a woman, shapely and dressed in revealing clothes, that is still considered the height of sex appeal in Italy. From Sophia Loren to Monica Bellucci, most of the successful Italian actresses are expected to fit that description and teenagers dream about them every day. Therefore, going out with a 'maggiorata' is every Italian (and non-Italian the writer dares to assume) teenager's dream.

Rovera

A small village on the hills outside Turin, the north-western Italian city - population just over a million - usually associated with Fiat and Juventus.

ROVERA - population three thousand - is where teenagers hang around the benches right outside the school, and right next to the only bar and playground. The benches, uncool as they may seem, are where many decisions were made in our story.

1989 – The year that changed the world

A key year in the history of Europe and the world. A year normally associated with the end of the Cold War, as during the summer student protests and other events facilitated the gradual collapse of the Berlin Wall, and the whole of the Communist Eastern Bloc in the following twelve months.

A lot of other things happened in this strange year, before mobile phones existed and when computers were as big as a car.

But the Berlin Wall, Solidarnosc in Poland and Tiananmen Square in China had a huge influence on the writer. A new era of hope was beginning, when everything seemed possible, and it was, as you are about to find out, and as you should know while reading this in 2021 post-Brexit and with Trump still a very vivid memory, everything, good and bad, is still very possible.

Prologue - The pear tree in our garden

1971. Italy was locked in the biggest economic crisis the world had ever seen. Yet that all seemed so far away from a small village near Turin, the Alps on the skyline and the sun shining most of the summer. In that small village, with only a few paved roads and no pavements to speak of. That was the year I was born, and my father planted a pear tree in our large garden.

Our brand-new house, built by my father and my uncle over eighteen months, was just completed. It was one of just a few houses on that winding country lane, leading only to fields - an elegant way of saying we were living in the middle of nowhere. It was new, and it was big, quiet and happy with spacious, airy rooms and two bathrooms - the ultimate luxury in those days. In fact, this was the most luxurious house the generations of my very working-class family had ever seen. Land was cheap back then, and for the first time in their lives my parents felt very smart in that large garden that looked more like a jungle than anything else.

My father was born in Veneto, where Venice is the capital, and he was an immigrant to the industrialised northwest, famous for Fiat cars. When he first arrived outside Turin in the late fifties, he had just finished fighting in the Second World War and could only speak his own dialect, therefore he was treated very badly by the local Piemontesi, who couldn't understand a word that the Veneti said. But my father wasn't the kind of man who gave in easily. Just a few years before he had been sent to a concentration camp in Germany. Yet he survived it and, when the war was over, he came back to Italy on foot. He was that kind of man.

He went to night school and, after long, punishing shifts, he improved his written and spoken Italian and he even taught himself the local dialect. He got both his diploma in Civil Engineering and his first proper job in a postwar Italy whose economy was exploding. He soon started working abroad. For twelve years he worked on big dams around the world, travelling to exotic places where no one else had ever been before, such as Egypt, Nigeria and Turkey. This at a time when the working class didn't even travel across Italy. For twelve years he lived on his expenses and saved the whole of his salary for the future - not really knowing what his future might be.

With those savings, while my mother was pregnant and they were expecting me, he bought the land and, with my uncle's expertise as a builder, built our house without a mortgage, paying in cash, and barely managing to finish it before all his savings of a lifetime were spent.

I was born when that new house was only six months old. The white walls were freshly painted, the garden still looked like a building site, and the road was barely a country path. But the view of the mountains on the horizon was wonderful from our windows, and it was that view they had bought. Even my grandfather came to live in the downstairs flat my dad had built for him for a few months, but Grandpa Ernesto didn't like the new house and it broke my father's heart when he went back to his old home in Veneto. My dad just wanted his own dad to be proud of him, but it wasn't meant to be.

After that, my father's heart would never break again until the Berlin Wall fell, but that is a story for later. When I arrived home as a week-old baby, my father was at peace again, and he then focused all the energies of his heart and soul on me, his only child.

To remind himself of that, being part of a generation brought up in the countryside in close contact with nature, he went out into the garden and planted a pear tree, his favorite fruit. He wanted a tree that would produce a lot of fresh fruit for his baby son every year so that I could enjoy it and grow into a strong, brave engineer, just like in his dreams. The 1971 summer was very warm, and the tree was full of flowers and buds, but when it came to fruit there was only one giant pear. Only one.

My father was perplexed and a bit incredulous. He had never seen such a thing in all of his 46 years.

The year after, he redoubled his efforts. More pruning, better manure from the farmer nearby. The tree still produced only one, even bigger, pear. 1.5 kg, so my father went to see the local plant expert, Duilio. From the same village in Veneto that he came from, the man to solve any practical problems. He came one Sunday morning at nine sharp, wearing his blue worker overalls and a beret, took one quick look at the tree and nodded thoughtfully. Then he went away and returned twenty minutes later with a bottle full of his special, secret plant medicine spray. He came back for three Sundays after that, always at nine, to spray the tree. Once the treatment was finished, they both waited until the following year.

Still only one pear. Even bigger. 3.7kg.

My father, being practical, was ready to cut down that useless tree that wasn't producing any fruit, even with Duilio's special help. However, that year I was an energetic four-year-old, keen to explore, and that strange pear tree in our garden was my favorite tree to climb. I started climbing its branches every day and I built a basic wooden hut around it. Very wary of disappointing his only son, my father was touched and decided not to cut it down. So, the tree is still there, and it gives one huge, delicious, sweet pear per year. Nothing less and nothing more.

PART 1 – May 1989 - Before the world changed

CHAPTER 1 - The world is collapsing around me, but I just want to celebrate my birthday...

May 1989. I'm eighteen! That's a very important year in our lives, right? And I have been waiting for this moment for so long. I shall be able to sell my old Vespa scooter, and if I do well at school my father will buy me an Aprilia Tuareg Rally motorbike. With that motorbike I will be a proper man. No more having to ask a hot girl to get off my Vespa to help me push it up on the hills of my village (true), no more 55 kph on the motorway around the corner and, most importantly, not always arriving last wherever we go. 1989 will be a magical year. I feel it. A year of adulthood and celebration. Another momentous step towards eventually being able to do everything I want.

We are in Northern Italy; the sun is shining, and it is May. My friends and I are at the Havana Bar, a Latin American-themed club with a terrace overlooking the nearby lake. Our friend Claudio, hair slicked back, is the party DJ. Fabrizio, tall, long hair, and permanent basketball-style Nike Airs on his feet, is chatting up a French girl – a friend of someone we don't remember. A crowd of friends bounce all around me. Lacking any imagination, we call ourselves 'The Bench Guys', because we always meet at some benches near the local schools. We live in a chocolate-box-pretty village near the Alps, but tonight this old Latin-American bar is the centre of my world. All the Bench guys and girls are ready to sing happy birthday to me. All our spotty faces are red from too much sangria, and hands with uneven nail polish hold bottles of cheap spumante. Everyone is ready to erupt on the terrace under the stars.

But stop!

Not quite. 1989 will be a year I shall never forget, but not for this reason.

Definitely not.

In less than one month we receive the end-of-year school results, and it is widely known that I shall fail my fourth high school year. Four failed subjects automatically make you fail the year. I have five. The head teacher Professoressa Pezzani comes to see me at the end of class and tells me how disappointed she is with me and that she expects my father, who cares so much about my grades, will be incredibly disappointed too. I smile. She is right. My father will be mad. But at the moment he does not have a clue and I want to keep it that way - until the last minute - so I can buy another month of peace and freedom after a very long year.

The issue is that I can't tell my father that his having a double heart bypass and my dreading he would die destroyed my concentration for half the year. Even if it was true, it wouldn't be the whole story. I failed because I wanted to. I decided that it was time for me to move away from this classroom of wonderful people where for too many years I have been the self-appointed class clown – and so I got used not to studying at all.

I've always been the guy who makes everyone laugh, but doesn't ever do any work. I've been the guy who pulls funny faces at the teachers, but at home I have a father who just wants to die. I can't tell my father that, when I thought he was dying, being the funny man took my mind off the possibility of becoming an orphan at seventeen. And I'm suffering in silence because my father has always been a tower of strength. My challenge. My enemy. Now how can he turn to me and ask me for strength? That can't be my responsibility now, right? I'm barely eighteen for Christ's sake... I can drive a car and tell you that R O I stands for Return on Investment, but I have no idea about life or making decisions. I don't know anything about being in charge. How could I?

Back in the corridor outside my class, severe Professoressa Pezzani nods less aggressively. I listen to her lecture calmly in silence, because I know that she cares. However, all I can think of while this old lady points her finger to me is that, at the end of the day, I am meeting Serena. Serena is the only reason why I'm going through this. A ray of sunshine in a world that turned all dark when I wasn't looking.

Professoressa Pezzani has stopped. I don't tell her that I was making everyone laugh because inside I was crying. Instead, I smile and say: "Thank you, you're right."

"Soriani. Go back to class. I think I've made my point," she says.

I agree. She has, and I've made mine. I go back to my desk in silence. All my friends are smiling. They know I've made the right decision and so do I.

27

A few days later, here we are at the Havana in suburban Torino, and as I celebrate my eighteenth birthday with my friends, I know my life is about to change forever. But as the spumante is uncorked and everybody screams happy birthday, all I can see is that Serena has gone off somewhere and is talking to Luca. Fucking Luca again.

Yes. You know. That Luca - tall, dark, handsome and with a permanent tan. The guy is two years older than us because he failed his year TWICE, making him too cool for school. He has a nice car AND a house by the seaside AND a father who sells sports cars for a living. A wonderfully profitable business that his lazy, smooth bastard of a son will obviously inherit, making him an instant millionaire in spite of his obvious academic failings - such is life.

On the other side of the Havana, me. I arrived with my unfashionable mother in her battered Panda. Not really tall enough. In clothes that never quite match everyone else's top brands. Our holidays are in unfashionable parts of Liguria and my skis are never quite the latest model. Should I complain? No, I really can't. I lead an easy, and some may say very middle-class and worry-free, life. My wise working-class parents have worked very hard to give me a hundred times more than they ever had. But I am very different from them, and they made me this way.

After ten years in the village, a lot of massive new houses have been built around ours. Suddenly our new neighbours are buying Porsches and building swimming pools. Our home doesn't look that impressive any more and growing up with parents like mine who can't help feeling inferior doesn't help either.

So at my own eighteenth birthday party, this is my most vivid memory: all I wanted to do was to pick up a bottle of spumante and break it over Luca's head. That would have made me extremely happy. But no. Unfortunately, I am not that kind of guy either. I won't kick up a fuss; I'd rather bow my head and feel I will win another day - whenever that may be.

This somehow fills me with the determination to manage a ferocious smile. So, I smile to celebrate, hug a few guys and kiss a few girls I don't even like. I smile. I laugh. I kiss. They kiss me back. They smile back at me. They sing my name. I feel alive. I feel good. Serena looks back, and just as I am starting to feel better, I see her kissing Luca.

"Evviva!" – "Happy birthday, loser!"

That night it's already dark when I get home. As I arrive, I realise I don't have the Swiss Bulova chronograph watch (worth about six hundred and fifty thousand lira, six hundred pounds in 1989) that my father had bought me for my birthday. In the heat of the moment and probably messing around to too much rock music, it must have dropped on the floor, and someone must have picked it up.

I never managed to tell my father, and I spent the rest of my life wearing cheap watches as a reminder, until I was almost fifty years old and capable of taking care of my things.

That night somebody drops me home and I walk in through the garage. The gate is open, as it used to be in those days: no one locked a gate back then. I sit down on the chair in the garage as I don't want my parents to see me this drunk. I sit there and our massive English sheepdog Pongo comes to put his big head on my legs. He lies down on my feet, as he's used to doing. I breathe in and breathe out. Drink some water and chew some gum. Then I'm ready to see my parents and pretend I'm not that drunk, and I didn't spend all that money just pretending to have fun.

To this day Professoressa Pezzani lives in the small town of Rovera. She is now seventy-five and her nephew came to the premiere of my first feature film in Italy... bringing me best wishes from his fierce auntie. This whole encounter gave me the acute sense of time flying by and the importance of just following your heart, one way or another. Even when you seem from the outside to be doing the most stupid things.

CHAPTER 2 - After I failed my fourth-year exams my father didn't speak to me for one WHOLE week

Our kitchen felt like a battleground that day. Succulent dishes of freshly cooked pasta lay untouched. The TV was switched off at one, when the 'Telegiornale', the daily news, was broadcast - unheard of. My mother tried to convince my dad to be less harsh, but he was just too disappointed and hurt. He is the 'pear tree' guy. He didn't imagine his only child, always smart and capable, a real academic talent, could ever, ever fail a year at high school. He used to go to high school after twelve hours of back-breaking work. He always passed his exams. How could his son, who had never worked a day in his life, fail?

I thought I would be able to say something smart as I always do, but when he was totally silent at the dinner table for three meals in a row I gave up. So, we ate in complete silence for the first time since I was born.

The TV news reported Tiananmen Square events and the disaster at the Heysel Stadium, where ninety-six Italian Juve supporters were killed by their Liverpool counterparts. New Cinema Paradiso triumphed at the Cannes Film Festival, but my father stayed silent throughout and that really freaked me out - especially since we are not exactly a quiet family.

There were only three of us, and so being quiet had always been an issue for me. I hated quiet and as a happy only child I used to fill that silence with pointless prattle. My parents were secretly proud of this obviously smart kid who read all the time and could never keep quiet. My father had already retired by then and was attending courses at the Adult Education Centre (as one does). Philosophy was his favorite course, and he would read the suggested books avidly just to keep busy and not go crazy with inactivity. That day he finished his meal in silence and, when the TV news ended, made for his Fiat Panda and drove off. Without a single word. Even ignoring Pongo who always followed him everywhere.

As he left, I found an excuse to say goodbye to my mother and I went downstairs to the garage and jumped on my Vespa. I started the engine up with a kick and I drove off. I only feel free on my blue Vespa though that's hard to explain. A feeling of freedom from a different world that is becoming more and more complicated every day. I take my helmet off and my then long hair - I so wish I had some left now - flies in the wind, light and free like I can never be, even for just a few moments. I take my hands off the handlebar as the Vespa goes downhill. Quiet, typical village sounds. The neighbours' TV. Somebody mowing the lawn. An old lady singing in dialect while she waters the flowers. This is my simple world - the only world I know and love.

On my way home again, I always go past the front of Serena's big villa. From faraway I can see the shadow of her having dinner with her family. Every night I stop for a few seconds on the other side of the road. I enjoyed looking at her from faraway. These were more innocent times, when a boy parking his motorbike on the side of the road wouldn't raise a terrorist alert. These were days before Facebook and Twitter. When people still talked to one another, and children went to school by themselves. I remember a few times when Serena came to the window and looked out, but I was invisible in the darkness of the street. She didn't know I was there. I knew. Somehow, I wondered how she would feel if she knew I was there waiting for a sign from her. Waiting and waiting, but she always ignored me. Someone better than me was more forthcoming and took the initiative, and I had yet to learn how to do that.

Luca's black Peugeot convertible roars to a halt outside her house, music full blast, braking at the last minute and leaving skid marks on their lane. The coolest car we all dream about, but only fucking Luca owns, stops in front of Serena's house. He uses the horn.

Che tamarro (*)! Serena's mother waves at him with a flirtatious smile from behind the curtains and then comes out. She likes him too. Luca lifts his Ray-Ban sunglasses and waits, and a few seconds later Serena waves goodbye to her mother and jumps into the car with him wearing the short green skirt I love. Her long blonde hair is done, and she has on that red lipstick I thought was only for me.

The car drives off past me, but they don't even notice I am there. Suffering in silence - as I do.

Yes. Serena just doesn't know I exist. And I wish I knew what to do about it, besides writing about her every day in my diary. Fully expecting her to break my romantic teenage heart, and not knowing that by the end

33

of summer I will break hers. No one would believe it now. Not even me.

(*) TAMARRO = punk/hooligan. Someone who has very poor manners.

CHAPTER 3 - Serena. And ME

Serena first appeared in my diary three years ago. It was May 1986, almost my fifteenth birthday and Fabrizio had asked me to go and watch a dance show at our local gym after our usual Saturday basketball match, just the two of us.

It didn't sound like my ideal thing to do on a Saturday afternoon. I was keener on playing football all afternoon on the tarmac pitch near the church, or even jumping on a mountain bike and riding across the beautiful hills that crown our village. Miles and miles of natural forest with jumps, mud and puddles. All the testosterone-fuelled body of a fifteen-year-old might want. The only reason I agreed to the basketball was because they told me that there would be a great view of Margaret's huge boobs. That sold it to me. Hey… I was fifteen, okay?

That day I walked past the old people's bar and said hello to Duilio, my father's friend who many years before had tried to fix our pear tree. It was kind of uncool to say hello to an old guy, but I felt I couldn't ignore Duilio - who would live to ride his bicycle up the hills until the age of eighty-six. Duilio was family, even if he could barely speak Italian and always, always spoke to me in Veneto dialect making me instantly uncool in front of my friends… but I didn't care.

What I didn't know until that breezy May afternoon was that the body of a fifteen-year-old also needs something else. That was going to be provided not by Margaret but by Serena - whom I didn't even know existed until that afternoon.

I locked my bike and walked into the local sports centre with my friend Fabrizio. I still remember the song hanging in the air. Whitney Houston singing 'How Will I Know.' I had never heard anything so exciting - or so loud for that matter. Chills went down my spine as the notes started rolling out in the corridor. I could feel my heart beat a bit faster. The expectation of what was to come felt like a shot of adrenaline straight into my small but growing heart. I could feel that my life was going to change forever. I've no idea why, but I just enjoyed that first 'slow motion' moment of my life. As they say - just like in the movies.

The Sports Centre was just a cavernous cement building, smelling of freshly cut plastic. These were the '80s when Italy was still wealthy, and we had a brand-new Sports Centre / Gymnasium, with basketball hoops that could be lowered from the ceiling by remote control. We sat on the decked cement steps around the main hall. It was only half full of doting mothers and younger sisters on one side and horny teenage boys on the other looking round to see what the fuss was about, every one of them with his eyes on a specific girl. I look around. Pretty much the whole village for our school year and two years below is here. Claudio, Fabrizio and I sit roughly halfway down the middle of the hall and the music keeps playing. Each of us has his eye on a different girl - as is the silent pact of boys in Italy. Girls come and go, but boy friendships are holy and meant to last forever.

Then suddenly a circle of twelve-year-old girls wearing very short blue skirts and white shirts and holding US-style pom-poms whizzes around the centre of the gym.

Time stopped.

That's just a cliché.

A blonde girl whom I had never seen before started dancing to the tune. The rest of the world disappeared in a fraction of a second. It was just me and her. She looked straight up at me, straight in the eyes. Her pouty lips sent me a kiss and...

...Then I came back to reality.

Reality was, sadly, rather different. The girl hadn't even noticed me. Her long blonde hair and beautiful eyes were all for another boy, Luca.

But from the next day I made damn sure she knew I was there!

Having watched American Graffiti and other popcorn films, I found every excuse to see her. To follow her. To make her understand that I was totally in love with her, and the fact that we were going to be together at some point. I made it feel absolutely inevitable.

I spent every hour of every day inventing new reasons to walk past her classroom - we were going to the same school after all - sit next to her on the bus - we were getting off at the same stop - pick her up for any reason to go anywhere she ever wanted to go - we had mostly the same friends - until she gave in.

Alone on a warm autumn evening on the steps of the sports centre where we first met, we kissed. Slowly, beautifully, innocently - more or less. It was magical, as it should be. Her beautifully shaped, very Mediterranean body wrapped around my gawky teenager frame, and I had absolutely no idea where my hands were meant - or allowed - to go. So, they just went everywhere winning me the nickname of King Octopus, which it took years to shed.

We were boyfriend and girlfriend for exactly seven days. I had achieved my purpose in life, I thought. My life was going to be so, so sweet. But no. It wasn't meant to be. After one week I understood why life can sometimes be horrible and complicated.

In spite of my absolute devotion, or more than likely because of it, she said after merely six and a half blissful days that she wasn't sure about her feelings, and she didn't want to go out with me anymore. So, she left me, saying she would miss walking the dog. I look at innocent, beautiful and extremely intelligent Pongo suspiciously with strong pangs of jealousy, and he barks gently to say: hey, it's not my fault.

I got to know the meaning of heartbreak for the first, but certainly not the last, time.

For about two days I was heartbroken as the news spread very quickly across the village. Strange things started to happen - first slowly, but then in a whirlwind -

so intense I could barely cope. Harsh world out there for young boys, isn't it?

Other boys were sitting next to her on the bus. Such is life, but there was an unexpected flip side.

Other girls seemed to be very keen on sitting next to me. And I was very happy for them to enjoy my company.

But somehow Serena stuck in my heart. She knew just how to attract me.

Maybe it was because we were going to the same school. Hanging around with the same people and going to the same parties. Maybe because of the walks with Pongo. We were always running into one another when she looked wonderful, and I was a mess in various stages of drunkenness and moodiness or both. In spite of whomever else we were with, somehow the flame was always there. I felt it. And I hoped she felt it too for three long, interminable years. Hard to let go. Hard to forget, but never quite enough to commit (on her side). We didn't have the adult wisdom of the years to come then. We didn't know some people are just not meant to be together.

After three years of growing up, getting taller, allegedly more mature, and focusing on ignoring each other while always making sure neither of us was going out with anyone else, I felt enough was enough and gave Serena an ultimatum.

It was an end-of-year party at our high school. All sorts of things were happening in our main hall. Everybody was dressed up and there was an unreasonable amount of alcohol being served. No teacher or parent in sight - of course. It was a windy day, and we were meant to go there together. She decided at the last minute that she didn't want to go with me. So that was the last straw. I took her aside.

As her gorgeous hair danced in the wind, I told her that I couldn't wait any longer. People walked by looking at us. We always used to bicker in front of everyone.

She told me she understood.

More people went by. More wondering looks as the wind got stronger and stronger.

I asked her what that meant.

Then the wind stopped. Right at that moment.

She said that she didn't know. She still couldn't understand her own feelings. She felt she didn't want to go out with me, but also didn't want to let me go.

Those blue eyes looked at me for the thousandth time, and she said with a seductiveness I am sure now she didn't even know she had:

"Is that crazy? Am I crazy?"

Those clear blue eyes stared at me for a moment too long. The red lips came a millimetre too close. I kissed

40

her there like I had kissed her so many times before. But before she could say another word, I stood up and left. That had never happened before.

"Where are you going?"

I didn't look back.

I went onto the dance floor, pushed Claudio and Fabrizio, who were wondering where the hell I was, away and went straight for the most overdressed girl in year twelve. I went straight for that stunning girl. The kind of girl whom on another day I would have never found the courage to kiss. The kind of girl who makes everyone else notice you. The girl who makes you popular. But I didn't care about anything. I just went ahead. And that girl (I don't even remember her name actually) knew it too. She kissed me nevertheless, and it was great. Only after the kiss I noticed she had braces so kissing her was like kissing a dead fish. However, I made damn sure that Serena didn't know any of this and, hell... wasn't she watching!

Everybody (!) was watching.

No one had ever seen me like that. What had happened to Alberto? Disruption! I could feel it. The whole school was feeling it. Maybe I had won. Maybe I had lost. But I knew I couldn't wait any longer and the hell with it.

One week later I got the answer: Luca and his impossibly perfect dark hair, chiseled looks and full-on tan, moved with his own Peugeot 205 GTI two houses down from her. He became her new neighbour.

Playground legend goes that she was walking to school when he spotted her, and told her straight away she was the most beautiful girl he had ever seen in his life. He also added that, that very Saturday he was going to pick her up. Allegedly she answered: "in your dreams." That answer made me smile. That was the Serena I knew - I thought.

Playground myths also report however that Saturday he did go and pick her up. They went to the cinema together, and my life instantly became a lot more complicated.

CHAPTER 4 - The Benches Guys – my world

As an only child, loneliness was always a killer. Loneliness in a small village in the countryside can be deadly. Those Saturday afternoons after a long week at school, and nothing is going on. Not a party, or if there is one you are not invited. An eighteen-year-old boy can go crazy.

It was this loneliness that brought me to writing. Just to stay sane. I didn't have very socially skilled parents who always had people around at home. So, I was often by myself with my ageing and very average parents who liked to spend the weekends working in the kitchen garden rather than going out to museums and art gallery openings like the younger, much cooler parents of all my richer friends.

Then I met Claudio and Fabrizio and my life changed. I had known of Fabrizio for a long time, but he was two years younger, so I didn't hang out with him. In him I found another maverick, if much more introverted and squarer than I ever was. A guy minding his own business and doing things his way. Like me, he was crazy about basketball and always desperate to go beyond what we knew, the village, the nation, life as we knew it. We shared a passion for London - one place where we knew we all wanted to go sooner or later. Fabrizio and I got to know each other over basketball games in the playground near Serena's home.

Claudio was different. Claudio was the life and soul of every party. Claudio was the DJ who loved cool music, the first to have any gadget, who always dressed smartly. The one with fleeting passions that lasted a few months in a never-ending sequence of purchases by his doting parents: vintage comics, Acid Jazz CDs, a DJ mixing deck, electric guitar, saxophone, mobile phone, Apple Mac, etc., etc., etc.

All three of us were only children. We did not have any brothers or sisters, but soon we had each other. Claudio of course was the connected one, the one who organised the group at the Benches. Fabrizio and I were the two misfits who were doing our own thing, but both of us must have been deeply lonely. We all saved each other from teenage boredom by hanging out with one another: three misfits outside the bar.

We soon became even more addicted than anyone else to hanging around at the Benches. The Benches were in a little park near the schools, the sports centre and a small bar, "Da Mimmo", aka "the old people's bar." All the kids hung around the Benches - rigidly divided by age: one bench for each year.

That Sports Centre was the essential part of every afternoon with never-ending basketball matches and colourful NBA balls. The old people's bar was the hub of every evening. The place where we started watching World Cup football matches and Formula 1 Grand Prix, and where we fought epic Super Mario Bros battles, each costing ten cents. It was a magical place with its simple plastic tables and chairs covered in bright plastic, where we started noticing girls were hanging around too… and suddenly we were going there every day.

It was still a very innocent time. We would go and play basketball and football. Then, slowly, BMXs became small motorbikes and, quickly, larger bikes and cars. People had parties there, barbecues, and later wedding receptions and christenings. Even now, thirty years later, some of those guys are still there barbecuing in summer. They look the same. They haven't moved very far from the village. Whether they are any happier than those of us who left to travel the world is debatable. The bar owner may be different now, but the furniture seems pretty much unchanged.

The Benches were also where we would write something to leave our mark. It would start with "Juve merda" or "Guns N Roses Forever."

But then it quickly became

'Sere I love you.'

Then,

'Sere stronza.'

Then even later,

'Sere senza di te non vivo.'

With all the group watching and shaking their heads. That was when the writing on the Benches stopped. The diary started to become more and more important. One

never-ending lonely summer's day at a time with just
my parents and Pongo.

PART 2 – June 1989 – The longest Summer of my life

CHAPTER 5 – I discover the cinema

That summer I suddenly discovered the cinema was my salvation from boredom. All I needed to do was to jump on my Vespa and abandon myself to the darkness of the room. Until then the cinema for me had always been social. I would go with friends.

But that summer for the first time I read some articles on the Cannes Film Festival, and I heard of this film called 'Do the right thing' by a new director called Spike Lee. It was meant to be the year of 'New Cinema Paradiso', and yet he became the first black director to win the Palme d'Or. The film would not be available in Italy until November but was already out in France. Our village is about one hour by train from France, so I decided to take a day trip and jumped on a train for France.

It was an unforgettable trip. Going all the way over the mountains just to watch a film. I didn't know it then, but that trip was going to change me forever.

Watching films became my obsession. The one thing that kept me sane.

My trip to France made history in our village. Some people in our village thought I was mad. Others thought I was very cool.

Girls started calling me up and noticing me at school. As the only real film nerd in our school, I found a niche I never realised I wanted. Interesting, nerdy girls started to gravitate towards me. The ones who watch a lot of films. The ones with glasses who hang out at the library - the quiet ones whom I hadn't noticed before. Some of them were actually quite good-looking. Some started to ask if we could go on film trips together. I said sure. It looked as though my infatuation with Serena would fade away after all, with the speed of a midsummer night.

Unexpectedly, one person who thought what I did was very cool also noticed the other girls and quickly made sure she had all my attention.

Serena.

Who knows? Maybe one day I may go to film school after all and make a film about this, I thought.

When I said this in front of my friends, they all laughed.

But Serena didn't laugh. She said: "You will, I know."

That was all I needed back then.

CHAPTER 6 - Serena and ME - And Luca

Serena and I meet one evening outside her house. My Vespa was parked outside the remote-controlled gate of her villa, and her dad's Porsche was parked just inside.

All the boys and girls from the Benches are going off on that fabled Interrail European trip very soon. A group of thirteen boys and girls, all seventeen and eighteen, will travel across Europe on a single train ticket. Serena will go, of course. And Luca too. Even Claudio and Fabrizio are going. I am the only one in the group who failed his year. I am the only one not allowed to go.

So, I am jealous, and she knows it. She asks me to write to her. I'm sure I will, however all I can think of is her and Luca in the same tent smoking a joint in Amsterdam under the stars. Maybe even sharing a tent. Just the thought makes me sick.

"Sere, but you and Luca…"

"Luca and I what?" she answers, prevaricating but also blushing.

"Nothing? I saw you the other night."

"And what did you see?"

"I saw… enough."

"So, you spy on me as well? You pervert," she says, and punches me jokingly on the shoulder.

"Well, you are going away in a few days."

"I know."

"And Luca? Is he going?"

"Of course, he is. But it doesn't matter..."

"It doesn't?"

A long silence. I can hear myself breathing faster. "No. It doesn't."

I stop breathing.

"Listen to me. Since you are not coming... I think it's important that we find a way of keeping in touch."

"Really?"

"Really."

"Why?"

She looks straight at me with those damn blue eyes again.

"In fact, you know what? I don't actually care why. Tell me how?"

"I will write to you."

"Yes, sure." I know she never will.

"I will send you a postcard from all the places we go to. One place, one postcard. Every day."

Silence. It sounded like a great way to keep in touch in a world twenty years before mobile phones.

"From every place?"

"I'll try my best, okay? I may miss a few days. If we keep in touch with one another after all this time... maybe when I come back, we'll be together. For real. If it's destiny, it's already yours."

"Sere, you've already told me that a hundred times and we split up after one week."

"This time I feel it's different. It's the summer of '89, remember. The world is changing. Have faith. Trust in love."

"Love... or whatever it is you feel," and she touches my chest briefly. "Here. Trust it!"

Her mother, dressed in designer clothes from head to toe, calls her from inside. She doesn't wave at me or at my blue Vespa.

"Coming, Mamma."

"Sere..."

"Yes?"

"When you see the Berlin Wall... especially if it's really true it's coming down... You have to send me some pictures. Ok?"

"If the wall is really coming down... I'll bring you a piece."

She smiles at me and kisses me on the lips.

I don't know if it's true, but I want to feel this kiss is different. That it tastes better and lasts a fraction of a second longer.

That night I go home and read my diary, checking the exact duration of previous kisses. Then, embarrassed, I switch off the light. As I lie down, I keep kissing my cushion in my dark bedroom, surrounded by all the books I've ever bought, and will reread one by one over the lonely summer days. That night as the light in the kitchen is switched off and darkness eventually envelops the whole house, I dream that my tongue still feels the sweetness of Serena. I hear Pongo howling outside. Even he knows how I feel tonight.

CHAPTER 7 - They Left!

They all left a few days later. Those were the longest two days of my life. I was trying not to call her every ten minutes. I was trying not to ask her every time if she really meant it. I tried desperately to hide my feelings and look cool. But I just couldn't. Then came the day of their departure.

They were meeting at Turin station, but a lot of them left with their rucksacks from our minuscule local station, four stops from Torino, just to feel even more adult. I couldn't go to the station. I didn't want to go. So, I stayed home, sweating.

Years later they told me that day I was incredibly moody. Years later she said the moment she realised I wouldn't go to the station to say goodbye was the moment she really fell in love with me. The moment when she wanted to jump off the train and come to my house to kiss me and God knows what else. But... she didn't.

So, I wouldn't know how she felt for at least another six months. That day all I knew was that she left. And that my life was going to be loneliness, boredom, the company of my books and three weeks of counting the days for her postcards.

I always say that you can never really understand how the heart of a woman works. But I was starting to realise that the safest bet is to always do the opposite of what logic suggests. That's served me well over the years - maybe. So, I stayed at home. They left. She left.

And my waiting summer of '89 was just beginning

CHAPTER 8 - The evening news talking about stuff happening around the world

That day felt as if the simple world that always made me happy was all gone. Dinner was tasteless. TV was uninteresting. Conversation was boring. On my walk with the dog after dinner, the blissful sunny countryside felt like a prison. My mind, and especially my heart, were elsewhere - on a train on its way to Paris. I felt stupid. I felt annoyed at myself and at my stupidity in failing the year. I said to myself it must not and cannot happen again. Even that is no consolation - everyone in my group has gone, and I am still here. All I can do is watch TV and pretend to focus on the evening news relentlessly showing what is happening in China. The first-ever student protest in that communist country. The magnitude of it overwhelms me, until in a few days, events become even more dramatic.

My dad and I watch TV together, but he is still upset with me. He doesn't speak to me. The old man has a soft heart though, and I know he will forgive me, but these last few days have been very hard. The world is changing, probably forever, and yet although it looks like the communist bloc is collapsing and the cold war is over, I can't stop thinking about how much I do not want to be at home.

The day of the Tiananmen Square events, my father stays up to watch the uninterrupted coverage with a sad face. He must be overcome by these events and by how the values that he has lived by and fought for in the Second World War are collapsing before his very eyes.

He walks slowly towards the phone and, with a heavy heart, calls both his brothers, Uncle Leonino, four years older and Nevio, four years younger than he is.

They spend an hour on the phone discussing Communism and how their dream is over. In normal circumstances that would have sounded like conversations between old people discussing meaningless stuff. But these were not average men. These men had fought in the Second World War and survived. My uncle Leonino was one of the survivors from the tragic Russian campaign, and my father had been deported to Germany and almost killed twice. These were men for whom Communism was an ideal they fought for with their lives. To ensure the world would never repeat what had happened in the Second World War. But these events in China made them all believe maybe their world was about to die. They agree to meet up the following Sunday at our house. My mother rolls her eyes and prays to the Madonna. Normally every single time the three brothers meet on a Sunday to talk politics they have massive arguments. Much as I love my uncles and my dad, I instantly make plans to disappear on a three-hour bike trip.

Honestly, I couldn't care less about China. I couldn't stand the whole discussion and went back to my room. Pretending to study, but actually just waiting for the postman to arrive with my first postcard - just as Serena promised.

Ah the reliable routine of the sleepy village in summer. Every day I eagerly wait for the postman's noisy grey scooter, which normally arrives at our house a quarter past twelve. So, on these warm summer days, I go and buy fresh bread at eleven every morning, and I'm home by twelve to wait for the postman.

"Alberto! Go and buy the bread, darling?"

"Not now, Mamma."

"Alberto!"

"C'mon!"

"I am not going to say it again. You're grounded!"

"Going, Mamma. Going!"

My traditional and very 'Queen Housewife' mother is getting lunch ready. This is a process that takes several hours every day as she cooks everything fresh, starting from the kitchen garden.

Bread is the last element to achieve perfection. Cooking in Italy is an art after all. She gives me ten thousand lire (plenty of money back then, around three euros today. But then it was very good pocket money) and I go up the road to the village shops on my Vespa. The bakery is only a kilometre from our home, and I could walk there, but I go by motorbike - of course.

We live in a tiny village of three thousand people that has two bakeries. Welcome to Italy. I go to the bakery we have used since I was born, and changing bakery is just not an option. Akin to changing political party or, even worse, changing football team. Our bakery is on the corner of the cobbled street leading to the church.

I park the Vespa just outside the tiny windows with fresh focaccia displayed nicely and a queue of people inside. As I open the door, the delicious fragrance of the hot bread just enfolds me. To this day it is one of my favourite smells in the world.

As I open the door I say: "Buongiorno."

Everybody inside choruses: "Ciao, Alberto."

Everybody knows you by name in a village like this. Everywhere you go you are bound to meet someone who knows you or, more likely, knows your parents. CCTV is not needed in a place like this. An army of bored ladies with nothing to do but to look out of their windows is just as devastatingly effective. Whatever you do, the whole village will know in a few seconds.

No more than ten people inside the shop. I queue up, wary of wily grandmas trying to skip the queue and jump ahead. It's hot inside the bakery in summer, but the warm smell of the bread and freshly made focaccia makes me feel at home. In summer when children don't go to school, every morning there's the same ritual. We queue, waiting for fresh bread to bring home to our mothers. The same faces. We all know each other. Nothing interesting or of note ever happens. I buy my bread. I pay and head back home.

As I go home on the Vespa, I pass Signora Vanessa, the Sophia Loren of the village, in her forties yet looking very good for her age, always extravagantly dressed in improbably tight-fitting dresses and just as improbable stiletto heels - only God knows how she keeps her balance on a cobbled road. I ride past her, and I admit, like every other man in the village, I glance. I have seen her a million times before of course, but today all I want to do is go back home and wait for the postman and the postcard.

I swear to God, for the first time in my life as I glance, I feel Signora Vanessa looking at me in a different way as she walks down from the bakery towards the newsagent.

She says: "Ciao, Alberto."

And I answer politely as always: "Buongiorno, Signora Vanessa."

And I drive away. Quick. Need to get back home.

That night the images of what is going on in China haunt my father and his principles of what the world should be like. What it means to be a communist and a man of the people. But really, I couldn't care less today. I love my dad and his principles very much. But not tonight.

I can see my father waiting for me to join him on the sofa to start another political debate. But, feeling a bit guilty, I give him a kiss and head back to my bedroom. I switch off the light a few seconds later. I hear the TV still on until very late into the night.

CHAPTER 9 - The postman eventually comes

The postman, Signor Carlo Azzaruti is small, chunky and has a long moustache. He smiles when he arrives. It's a small village in Italy after all and we've had the same postman since before I was born. He knows us by name too. He knows what our motorbike engines sound like, just as we know and recognise his.

His, because of a pierced exhaust pipe, sounds louder than usual. "Paaahhhhh prom prom." Until he stops.

When the postman stops to drop off the mail, he leaves the engine running.

"Put put put."

A few seconds to put the mail in the box, then "PAAAAAAHHHHHHHHHHH" as he rides off and the sound becomes fainter and fainter in the distance.

I breathe in and breathe out. The moment has come. From my window I can see that the lid of the postbox is open. Something is inside for sure. It could be a stupid letter from school, or it could be her postcard.

I want to run, but I walk slowly.

"Mamma, I'm going down to get the mail."

My mother ignores me and focuses on food. That is her raison d'être, together with her crazy only son.

"Sure…"

I go down the steps of our two-family-villa three at a time. I make a lot of noise. My uncle who lives downstairs will surely complain, but I don't care as I walk to the postbox. I can already see that there is a postcard. I'm there. I don't want to look at it, so I just glance at the picture.

Day 1 - post card 1 - Lione

I can't believe it. She's really done it!

My heart beats like crazy. I go into the garage for some privacy - followed by Pongo, but when I close the door of the Panda and the dog barks at me, I have to let him in and sit on the passenger seat.

There it is. The first postcard, Serena's rounded writing is unmistakable. She writes very well.

"Ciao bello."

(Bello? - does she really mean 'handsome' it or is it just a manner of speaking?)

"Qua tutto bene."

(What does that mean? She's sharing a tent with Luca? Or…?)

"Baci,"

"Sere xxx"

I smile. C'mon! Is this it? What does she mean 'All is well here?'

There is hope. Or is there?

Pongo looks at me unsure of what's happening. I let him out and then slam the door.

I waited for one week... for this?

CHAPTER 10 - Day 2 - If an Italian goes to pick up the bread... he goes every day at the same time. Fact.

Italians like their habits. We are the stalwarts of tradition and do not like change.

We wake up. We hug. We kiss (at least in my family). We always kissed each other every morning. I kissed my mother and my father every day until I buried them both. I was the last one to kiss them and send them on their way to the next world. After a healthy dose of kissing and hugging, we eat breakfast every day, a caffe latte and a sweet brioche. Normally a choice of the three. Then, at least in summer when school is out, I pretend to do my homework and then... there you go. Guess what happens next? Buying the bread. Fresh bread again, sometimes even walking the dog. I go up at the same time and Signora Vanessa crosses my path again.

This time I pay more attention. She is wearing an orange dress and very, very high-heeled black sandals. Everyone in the village knows that Signora Vanessa changes her outfit every day, and they say she never wears the same outfit twice. As a generous proportion of her exuberant cleavage makes its way into the bakery, every man looks and every woman curses. Yet everybody also knows she goes to the newsagent every day to buy Il Sole 24 Ore, the famous and unmissable, orange-coloured financial paper. The idea that such a good-looking and apparently shallow woman is also into finance and investment is the source of never-ending gossip. It is a village of only three thousand people after all.

I can't help admiring the balls she must have to dress that way in a village like ours. The women clearly hate her, but they pretend not to. The men watch and admire, but are too intimidated to chat her up under the eyes and tongues of a thousand wives who meet every Wednesday at the market in the square near the church.

I buy my bread and look at her cleavage again on my way home. She notices, and looks away with a knowing smile, the kind of smile that says: "I know you looked." I ride back to wait for the postman.

No card today.

Signora Vanessa's suggestive smile floats gently in my mind somehow, trying to work its way into the sea of images of Serena. Serena smiling, Serena alone. Serena with me. But then I can't help having visions of Serena and Luca in France, Serena and Luca holding hands in Spain, Serena wanting to write me a card and Luca ripping it in half in Portugal. In the middle of these thoughts, just out of nowhere, I weirdly think about seeing Signora Vanessa again tomorrow. I have no idea where that thought came from. Maybe, as I am studying business myself, I will ask her about the stock market?

But the thought stays there. It doesn't go away. I stand up and go to the kitchen. I check that all the bread left in the cupboard is finished. I smile. My mum is planning to go shopping in the afternoon in her red Panda. She asks if I want to come, and I say of course.

CHAPTER 11 - Day 3 - Post Card 2 - Paris

I go and buy bread and Signora Vanessa is not there today. I'm a bit disappointed as I was looking forward to checking out her outfit, so I head home to even worse news.

PARIS

I turn the card over, expecting epic poetry, and all I can see is a small 'BACI' (**) in the corner.

Then everyone's signatures.

Everyone's. Including Luca's.

WTF? Why did she think I wanted Luca's signature on the card?

I look in the mirror and hardly need to ask myself if she still cares. I know the answer.

God. Why do girls have to be so complicated?

And I jump on my Vespa and go looking for consolation in the summer emptiness of the deserted village. I feel I can find it in only one place.

(**) Kisses

CHAPTER 12 - Day 4

Those cobbled streets again. Consolation. Relief and revenge today mean bread.

That is how pathetic I feel as I go up and down the main street of the village waiting for Signora Vanessa to leave her flat in the big block on the main road for the bakery and/or the newsagent.

I am impatient and my heart is in tumult and, as one might expect under these conditions, Signora Vanessa is taking her time. C'mon, why do you have to make me wait?

But today Signora Vanessa is walking down the road as I get to the bakery. It is very hard not to look at her as she is wearing a red dress so tight that it looks like it could explode at any time. And the way she walks... very, very hard not to look.

This is a woman who knows how to attract male attention, and she is used to every man looking at her. So, I try to not to look too hard. Why? I don't know. Am I actually meant to look? And if I am... where do I look anyway? Yet, intriguingly, I notice the financial papers in her bag. So, it must be true. There is definitely more to this woman than meets the eye.

All these thoughts spin faster and faster as she gets closer. My confidence drops lower and lower. My teenage shyness reaches maximum level, yet as I see how deep her neckline is today, Signora Vanessa notices, smiles and answers all my questions.

She looks at me. Straight into my eyes. She has beautiful green almost purplish eyes, like the famous Elizabeth Taylor. I look down and blush. She smiles again and says: "Buongiorno Alberto."

"Buongiorno Signora."

"Come stai?" she says...

Me? I stop and look at her from a metre away. She stops and looks at me too. I wish I could say something amazing, but all my focus is on keeping my eyes straight on hers as opposed to lowering them to her cleavage. It is a superhuman effort, but I just about succeed.

"Bene grazie." I am desperately looking for something to say, but am about to give up and run off when she says: "Do you like my dress?"

Did she really ask me that? I have no idea why this woman gives me palpitations, but she does. I am not sure why she stopped and looked at me that way, but I really admire the way she looks today.

"I made it myself, you know. I make all my dresses myself..."

I look up and down at all those curves - pretending to look only at the dress...

"They are very n-n-n-nice..."

"Thank you. You are a very polite young man. I shall see you tomorrow then? I buy the newspapers every day..."

I am so curious I can't resist: "Which newspaper do you read, Signora?

"Il sole 24 ore - the financial paper."

I smile. It's true.

"Do you follow the market?"

"I do. Very much so... So should you."

"I am studying business at school."

"Great. So, we'll have plenty to talk about..."

And off she glides in her red dress. Fully aware I am paralysed by the view and that my eyes are glued to her. She walks away to the bakery slowly. I stand in the middle of the little alley, watching. As she goes in, she turns back. Looks to check if I am still there. She waves with the papers in her hand, as if to show me she really does read the financial papers. Then, effortlessly, she walks into the bakery.

Don't ask me why, but that night in my diary I describe her outfit in detail, something I have never done until now. You only see that kind of outfit on pinups on television, probably on one of those horrible Berlusconi channels I can only watch when my father falls asleep.

I write out a few notes:
Red dress - huge slit
Black heels
Neckline - low, tight bra, one size too small?

Then I switch off the light. I wake up again. I go to the kitchen where my father keeps the newspapers we read. And, for the first time in my life, I read the business news. I try to find it interesting but... it doesn't last long.

As I switch off the light, an incredible thought strikes me.

Oh my God. I switch the light on again.

I didn't check the postbox.

My mother is sleeping soundly and snoring, but my dad is still up. The light from the TV illuminates the kitchen. Well, my dad is sleeping while another program on politics has ended and been replaced by late night adverts for strip clubs. My dad and his dirty secrets are safe with me. I switch off the TV though before my mother wakes up and slaps him.

As soon as I switch off the TV my father wakes up.

"What did you do that for? I was watching!"

I switch the TV back onto the late-night adverts for a porn star called MOANA.

"Were you watching this?" I ask cruelly.

My dad looks embarrassed, but only for a few seconds.

"Why did you change channels? What do you take me for?"

I laugh. He takes himself very seriously and he is very aware of his standing as the head of the family with almost regal pomp. The King of the family can never ever be found out so, he doesn't actually laugh at all. In the end, he can't help himself.

"You're right. Buonanotte but go to bed. It's late. And you? What are you doing still up?"

"Have to go downstairs to check the mail."

"Now? Are you mad?"

"Two minutes…"

"Serena again? I don't know what you like in that girl… You know I heard strange rumors about her dad?"

"Don't listen to gossip, Papa. That's what you taught me."

I go down the stairs slowly. I get to the gate and unlock the letterbox.

But before I get there, I know that there is nothing in it. I feel it.

I open the letterbox anyway and stare at its emptiness and at what it means.

My dad is keeping an eye on me from the window. He is wondering if I am going insane and I probably am.

I look up at the quiet summer sky. It's dark, but shining with light, and for the first time I only think for a few seconds of what the sky must look like in northern Europe.

As I get back my father calls me.

"Yes, Papa."

"I think you are wasting the summer. Not studying, not doing anything."

"Papa, I failed my year..."

"Yes. Thanks for reminding me. At your age I was..."

"Studying after working all day and getting top marks. Not like me. Obviously."

"Exactly..."
Then this burly man touches my face delicately.

"I don't want you to waste your life. I think a bit of real work would do you good."

"Fine, Papa. I don't mind at all."

"You could make some money too, you know."

"That sounds good too."

"All right. I'll ask around tomorrow."

"Thank you, Papa. Thank you for not giving up on me."

"You are my son. How could I possibly give up on you?"

"You never know..."

"When I was sick last year... You didn't give up on me. You helped me to not give up on myself. It wasn't easy, you know. It was your smile that kept me going."

"Papa..."

"Yes?"

"I beg you. I never want to hear you wishing yourself dead. No matter how hard it may be. Stay with me, okay? I need you."

"Don't worry. I'll hang around for so long that you'll get sick of me."

"Papa…"

"Sì?"

"When Uncle Leonino and Uncle Nevio come on Sunday…"

"Yes?"

"Can you promise me you won't argue too much?"

"Alberto. We are brothers. We don't argue. We only… exuberantly exchange opinions."

"Ok. Promise me you will 'exchange opinions' in a very calm way. Will you promise me?"

We both chuckle. My father is shorter than me now, and forty-six years older than my eighteen. He kisses me on my forehead like he always does and says: "I promise."

CHAPTER 13 - A Sunday and 'CALM' Political Debate

When my uncles and their wives come to visit my father, it is a special day. They always come after lunch. My mother starts preparing snacks early in the morning. My father reads the newspaper in more detail than usual to make sure all his facts are correct. He invites his brothers to discuss politics, but he definitely likes to prove himself right.

I stick to my plan of ensuring the dog doesn't jump on the guests, and leave as soon as possible afterwards. Even if there is nothing to do and no one to go off on a bike trip or to swim in the river with, I'd rather be alone with Pongo than listen to all these normally lovable men shouting at each other.

My uncle Leonino is a character. He is the eldest brother and therefore technically the head of the family, tall and elegant with a full head of white hair. His wife is Auntie Norma who will live to almost a hundred. Uncle Leonino famously survived the disastrous Mussolini campaign in Russia (something mentioned in every conversation) and always arrives early in his green Fiat 128. He parks on the corner outside our house and always brings pasticcini, a delicious typically Piemontesi Sunday treat: small cakes in different shapes, glazed or covered with fruit and filled with cream, chocolate and pistachio. Just looking at them makes you fat. But back in those lovely days, no one cared, and cholesterol and diabetes only happened to other people.

They ring the bell. They go and say hello to my other uncle downstairs and then eventually make their way to us. We kiss. We hug, and they come to the living room - as guests of honor, as normal, less special guests would come to the kitchen. When we use the living room, we know the visit is important. They ask me if I have a girlfriend, and when I say no, my uncle looks at my dad, and my dad looks at the ceiling...

My uncle looks back at me and I smile. I know what's coming...

"Alberto... A good-looking boy like you... What's going on?"

"Nothing to worry, Uncle. I'm on it..."

"Alberto... he lowers his voice conspiratorially... it's all working down there, isn't it?"

"Yes, Uncle, it's absolutely fine."

"Alberto, you know I survived the campaign in Russia?"

No, not again, Uncle, please... but my Auntie Norma saves me...

"Leonino, leave the boy alone... we've heard the story of you in Russia a million times. Come, Alberto, have some pasticcini..."

My uncle protests meekly but sees that his moment in the spotlight is past.

"I just wanted to say that... a man needs to be able to suffer sometimes..."

My father jumps in...

"His time to suffer will come, brother. Now let him have fun for another few years... one day he will learn..."

"Alberto, come here. Sit with us."

"Grazie, Zia."

"Vieni, vieni, have some cake... a glass of wine?"

"Of course not. He doesn't drink – yet" says my mother innocently, blissfully unaware of the many parties I've been drunk at since I turned fifteen.

Italian women of that generation - whenever there is a problem, they feed you. You may end up fat, but you will be happy.

Maybe because of this, and the habit of showing and expressing emotion, Italy has always had one of the lowest suicide rates in the world. We may not be efficient, nor successful, but we have a beautiful country - 75% of the natural beauty and art in the world - and we are happy. So, it's not a bad deal after all.

My uncle Nevio arrives soon afterwards. He is my favourite uncle - even smaller than my dad, but less chunky. He is two years younger and has a fiery temper - just like the other two. He is married to my Auntie

Giannina, the most elegant woman in the family, who talks very slowly and always takes great care of herself.

Uncle Nevio and Auntie arrive with more pasticcini and everybody sits down around the octagonal living room table. A bottle of wine is already in the centre of the table. A glass each. The ladies would prefer a Cinzano aperitif, so my mother goes to get it. The coffee is ready, and the uncles smoke MS cigarettes.

Uncle Nevio and Auntie Giannina always arrive with presents for everyone. That's how they are, and their children will carry on the tradition. To this day we spend Christmas together.

"So piccolo (***), how are you doing at school? What happened this year? I thought you were doing so well?"

(***) piccolo = little one

Uncle Nevio although I am already a head taller than he is, always calls me 'little one' because I am the youngest of my generation of children.

My dad rolls his eyes. This is a subject he never wants raised again.

"Uncle... what can I say? It was bit of a weird year. So much stuff happened."

"Don't blame me again, ok?" says my dad.

Uncle Nevio always defends me.

82

"But you have to admit, Remigio, that your illness must have an effect on the poor boy, no?"

"Grazie, Uncle..."

"All excuses, Nevio. He just didn't study hard enough..."

"But I'm sure he will be fine next year, won't you, Alberto?"

"I will, Uncle. I have time this summer to revise..."

"No holiday?"

My father gets annoyed now.

"Holiday? He failed his year at school... and I should send him on holiday? Studying is his job! The only one he has."

"Give the boy a break, Remo. We've all been through quite a lot this year."

I stare at my dad...

"Thank you, Uncle..."

Uncle Nevio made me appreciate the importance of bringing presents to young kids if you want them to be happy to see you as adults. Kids, after all, always listen to the relatives who play with them.

I eat a couple of pasticcini, grab a coffee, and while they're still talking amicably, I try to excuse myself.

"Ok, guys. Great to see you and I'm off now..."

But it's not going to happen. Uncle Leonino tries to rope me in.

"Are you going already? I haven't seen you for such long time... We need to talk about girls..."

"Leave him alone, Leonino. He is a Soriani after all," says my father "He knows what to do, right, Alberto?"

I look at my dad with a puzzled smile. It's very unlike him to defend me like that ...

"Uncle, I just have to meet... a friend..."

My uncle looks at me, genuinely worried "A girl, right?"

Everybody looks at me...

"Of course, Uncle. I am... erm... going to a girl's home. We have been planning this for the whole week. Her parents are away, so..."

Uncle Leonino stands up. "Bravo, Alberto. Now we're talking... Go conquer!"

I stand up and walk out. My dad pours another round of red wine. As I head out the door, I can already hear voices rising the minute the word communism is uttered. Time to go.

My mother follows me to the door.

"Alberto…"

"Sì?"

"You aren't really going to meet a girl, are you?"

"Mamma, they're all away on holiday. I just want to get out of here fast, before it all kicks off…"

"I don't blame you. I wish I could leave too. Take Pongo with you, ok? He needs a run."

Out of the corner of the eye. I can see my father standing up and he's raising his voice again. His brothers are not backing down though.

"Of course. Ciao, Mamma. I'm going."

I disappear off to the fields with Pongo. I ride my Vespa all around the countryside, the dog running alongside me. Without a helmet, I feel the warm air on my head. I lie down in a field, sunbathing and letting the wounds of jealousy heal as the dog runs around nearby. I don't know where Serena is or what she may be doing. I feel at peace, and I fall asleep in a field, listening to my music on the Walkman and sharing our bottle of water.

The hours go by. When the sun sinks, I wake up with the Pongo dog asleep by my side. He has the most accommodating temperament ever. I hug his big head and he licks my face. This is just what I need today. We get ready to go back home.

The minute I get back home and switch off the music I can hear shouting through the open windows.

My uncle downstairs is on the balcony...

"C'mon, Alberto, go and tell your father he can't scream like that... I wanted a siesta, but they've been screaming like this for three hours... it's unbearable."

Across the street the neighbours are watching, expecting a big fight. This is Italy after all; people scream all the time - and not necessarily just when they are angry.

I go upstairs ready to find mayhem, but I just see three men, all red in the face from too much wine, arguing furiously with each other about which is the most hardcore communist. As one does.

The wives have given up and are sitting separately in the kitchen and talking calmly about non-confrontational stuff, obviously tired of their husbands and the shouting. My mother calls me.

"Alberto, go and say something to your father. They've been like this for two hours now..."

"Ok, ok..."

I go into the living room, and they stop talking for a second. My father looks at me with a smile, while his brothers huddle around him.

"Alberto, put him to bed... he's had too much to drink."

"What are you talking about, Nino? You know I'm right..."

Both his brothers roll their eyes.

"Remo, you are always right - in your head. But no one ever agrees with you. Alberto... tell him..."

"What do you want me to say?"

"Do you agree with your father?"

"I don't know what you guys are talking about..."

"That Communism is dead, and sooner or later all these walls will fall and Europe will be unified. Maybe the whole of Europe will be part of the EU..."

"I don't know, but certainly something is going on. My friends are in Berlin at the moment."

"And?"

"Well, from what they are saying the Berlin Wall is coming down."

"Rubbish", says my father. "I'm sure they've smoked too many joints."

"Papa, they even sent me pictures... Apparently in the next letter..."

"Remo," says Uncle Nevio, "just because you refuse to believe something is happening... that doesn't mean it's not happening..."

My father starts shouting again and the bell rings... silence for the first time.

It's my other uncle from downstairs, my mother's brother outside our door.

"Have you shouted enough for today? I've been trying to sleep since half-past two and it's almost five ... Can you give us and the rest of the neighbourhood a break? No one really cares about your communism anyway, you know. What is meant to happen, will happen. You have no power to stop it..."

The three brothers look at each other for a second. Then they look at my uncle.

"Fernando, what you just said is very deep. Come and have a glass of wine..."

No need to say all the uncles stayed for dinner and left around ten, driving very, very slowly.

Drink-driving was another one of those words no one had invented yet.

CHAPTER 14 - A few days later

DAY 5 POST CARD 3 - Brussels - Thinking of you
XXX

Orange dress.
Black slingback heels.

DAY 6 nothing

Red skirt and white shirt
High slit on the side
Black patent shoes.

DAY 7 nothing

Flowered white and green dress. Green sandals.

DAY 8 POST CARD 4 - Berlin. - How's life? XX Will
send you pictures of the wall when I see it... Not that
straightforward after all...

And it's there that it happens:

"The Berlin Wall is coming down, they say. But at the
moment it seems to be holding up. Solidly."

My father is in front of the TV. Watching. While students and young people are kicking the Wall down. It
looks like it really will happen. My father goes to his
bedroom. Comes back into the kitchen (we only have
the TV on in the kitchen) and opens a little Chinese lac-

quered box. It contains all his Communist Party membership cards, dating back to 1964.

My father's eyes are moist, but he would never admit it. He's not that kind of man. He looks at me solemnly and says: "From today on, no more Communism. That's it."

"But, Papa, you know my friends are going to Berlin. They may bring me a piece of the wall. They promised."

"If they do, I will burn my Communist party membership card on top of it - to officially admit my ideals, which I fought for in the Second World War, have failed. But I hope the Wall will not fall. The Wall is a symbol. We tried to build a different life. At least we tried. Capitalism is not the only way to live, you know?"

"Papa, I'm with you. You know that."

Then my father walks down to the kitchen garden and goes back to his vegetables, which he tends with as much care as he takes care of me.

And as my father refashions his fall of Communism blues into taking care of his tomatoes, the whole world watches Berlin and, by association, my cool friends who are there. In the place that today is the centre of attention of the whole world.

I, in my ridiculous village in the middle of nowhere, receive this card.

"BERLIN

Hi Alby. I'm not sure what is happening here, but for the first time in my life I feel at the centre of the world. The village seems so very far away. And you too. I do not know how I feel. Maybe I think I don't want to come back. I'd like to stay here. Forever. What a strange life. But I miss you. And sometimes I don't.

Here they say the Berlin Wall is falling. That it's going to come down soon. This wall has divided people for fifty years, and yet everybody here feels that it is coming down and Germany will be united again. This gives me a lot of energy. Maybe everything is really possible in life. Even in our lives.

I don't know what this means now, this summer. But simply... don't wait for me. It wouldn't be fair.

As I promised, I have a
piece of the Berlin Wall for
you.

I am not sure you have it in
you to wait for it - or for me.

Baci e abbracci (****)"

The world as we know it is collapsing around me,
and I am collapsing too. My father tells me that in his
relatively long life (he is almost seventy) he has never
experienced anything like the fall of the Berlin Wall. I
feel the same. But I am not sure that is necessarily a
good thing.

That night I don't sleep well. I wish I could ring
Serena tonight. I wish I could speak to her. It is on
nights like this that all Signora Vanessa's outfits fade
into insignificance. But with Serena away for another
two weeks that is all I have to hang on to in my lonely
summer nights. I don't know why, but I can't suffer
alone. I want to suffer with someone, and this older
woman is all I have to fight this creepy feeling that
come September Serena will ignore me again - just like
in the past three years. And perhaps I have waited long
enough. Is it time to move on?

Can everything happen in life? Can the Berlin Wall
fall? Can people really change the world? Can true love
become reality?

A few hours later, like a very well-behaved Italian boy, I ask my father, who is watching the late-night news - as always half-asleep on the sofa:

"Papa?"

"Yes?"

"They say maybe the Berlin Wall will fall. Do you think it is possible?"

"Who says that?"

"Serena. She's in Berlin right now with all our friends."

"What the hell do they know? The Wall will stay there. As an example of the power of Communism. The Wall will outlive Serena and all her stupid friends."

"Okay. Good to know. Goodnight."

"Goodnight, my son. Don't worry about this. Whatever happens in the world, your dad will be there to take care of you."

I go and hug this rugged old man with a heart bigger than the whole world.

"You know, Papa, one day I hope I will be like you."

My father looks at me and smiles. Surprised at this tender moment with his hormonal teenage son, who most of the time spits out hatred.

"Remember, I don't want you to be like me. I want you to be better than me. Otherwise, what's the point?"

Not easy, my dear Papa. Not easy.

(****) Hugs and kisses

PART 3 – July 1989 – The encounter you couldn't possibly expect

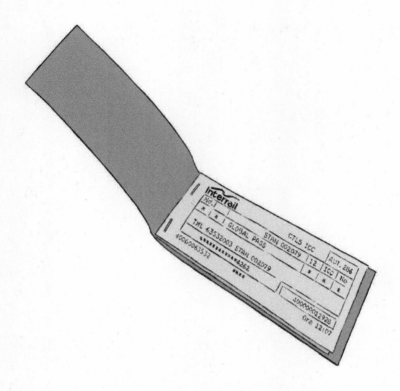

CHAPTER 15 - Signora Vanessa on a bicycle

I jump on my Vespa and drive off. Just as I always do when I feel like this. If the world is coming to an end and nothing makes sense, there is salvation in riding your Vespa along these small roads. It's soothing to head up to the hills, to the forest, until the road ends and it becomes a track, going up and up and looking at the view. The mountain behind and the pond nearby. Calm, and total silence.

Only then, from underneath my helmet, I let go of what has been in my stomach ever since I read that fucking postcard.

I release a very heartfelt...

Biiiiiiiiiiiiiiiiiiiiiiiiiitch!
Oh!

I repeat it over and over again. And again. Screaming louder and louder.

Biiiiiiiiiiiiiiiiiiiiiiiitch!
Biiiiiiiiiiiiiiiitch! Biiiiiiiiiiiiiiiiiiiiiiiitch!
Biiiiiiiiiiiiiiiiiiiiiiiitch! Biiiiiiiiiiiiiiiitch!
Biiiiiiiiiiiiiiiiiiitch! Biiiiiiiiitch! Biiiiiiiiiiiiiiitch!
Biiiiiiiiiiiiiiiiitch!
Biiiiiiiiiiiiiiiiiiiiiiiiiiitch! Biiiiiiiiiiiiiiitch!
Biiiiiiiiiitch! Biiiiiiiiiiitch! Biiiiiiiiiiiiiiitch!

Now I feel better even though I still wonder...

"Why do I care so much?"

I ride back down to the village, through the empty alleyways. There is no one in the street. It's hot and people are inside.

And then I see something that doesn't make any sense at all but is about to change my life.

Signora Vanessa riding her bike. Said like this it's not very exciting.

Yet the issue is... Signora Vanessa being... Signora Vanessa. She is riding her bicycle in a blue dress and black heels with a neckline that shows a very large part of her ample cleavage and a slit that shows all her legs. Something inside teenage me clicks.

Today is the wrong (or right?) day for this to happen.

If it were yesterday, I would never even have thought about it. But today as she zips downhill, I find myself turning the motorbike and chasing her down the main road. I don't know what I am doing or even what I am going to say. All I know is that today I don't want to think about the postcard that has just arrived to lacerate my fading hopes.

I catch up with Signora Vanessa, who glances at me, and smiles as she recognises me.

"Careful with that bike, Alberto."

"Yes, no problem."

Silence…

"May I say one thing, Signora Vanessa?"

"Sure…"

Silence… A thunderstorm of thoughts swirls through my mind. Current affairs? Politics? Even the stock market? Anything, just to make an impression… But what comes out is:

"May I say you have the most beautiful legs I have ever seen?"

I mean, seriously - emojis had not been invented back then, but I so wish I had had the one covering its face….

W T F. REALLY??????

Of all the things that you could have said… You, gigantic, supersize, gargantuan loser - you said that?

I can already imagine her getting off the bike and slapping my face.

Never wanting to talk to me again.

Yet she turns towards me and, somehow, she smiles!

"Well. What can I say? Thank you."

I ride next to her just admiring all those shapes and not really sure what I'm going to do next. She decides for me as we reach a nearby block of flats and cut across towards her gate. She gets off the bike and parks it near the gate.

I just stand there and look. Not sure what will happen next.

She looks at me and simply goes to her glass front door. She opens it with a key. I keep staring. Maybe I should follow her? Do I look like a stalker? Is her husband going to come down and beat me up? Or...?

"I live here."

"Great."

"Well then, see you again. Arrivederci."

"Arrivederci."

I'm ready to go. I've already turned around. Upset with myself for never being able to find the right words in situations like this. The words always come five minutes later, when full-flowing thoughts and perfectly formed seduction techniques appear out of nowhere. But at the time, when I need them most, my mind is blank as I walk away, ready to slap myself.

"Alberto?" she says.

I am actually surprised she wants to talk to me again. My heart skips a beat. I turn much more slowly than I intend. Just to stay cool. To try and hide the tumult I really feel inside.

"Call me," she says.

She turns around and walks through the gate. The way she walks would make a grown man tremble. Imagine what it does to an eighteen-year-old virgin. As I tremble like a useless jelly, she gives me one last look and winks before disappearing up the stairs.

No need to say that night was the first time in my life I felt an irresistible need to disappear to the bathroom. After I had spent thirty minutes on the toilet, my poor, wonderful, innocent mother thought I was sick. I wasn't sick-sick. I just felt an incredible rush of emotion and adrenaline like I had never felt before. I certainly wasn't in love, but if I wasn't in love... what was it?

CHAPTER 16 - Dominated by new-found LUST, my days changed - radically

Instead of counting the days to a postcard, I had suddenly found a new reason to keep track of time: Signora Vanessa's incredibly seductive outfits.

I couldn't believe I was doing that, but I couldn't stop either. It was totally addictive, totally exciting - an incredible urge I had never felt before. Something that made me forget everything. The fact that my father seemed ill again. That Serena had disappeared for five days without a trace. The fact that I had actually failed my year and my life would have to change come September.

But for now, I could only think about Signora Vanessa and her outrageous outfits, clearly designed to turn me on, clearly worn to tease and attract my attention, barely covering a voluptuous woman who was just a few years younger than my mother and who probably had a husband and, God forbid, a son my age. But in my sleepless nights none of that mattered. All that mattered was the dream. The idea of actually holding that dream woman and all her pin-up curves in my arms.

Little did I know I was going to discover her heart. But not yet. As the telephone rang that night. Very late.

CHAPTER 17 – Fabrizio's late-night phone call

It surprised, but didn't shock me. They were in Portugal now. The group had split up, and Fabrizio was with Serena's part of the group, of course. His familiar voice sounded like heaven. I needed a friendly voice on a night like this. When I should have been thinking of them... but actually wasn't. The voice of one of my best friends brought me down to earth. Where I should still belong. Somehow.

And Fabrizio tells me all about their holiday. He is very descriptive, Fabrizio, and wastes a lot of time on incredibly pointless details - such as the colour of the tent and the sound of the birds in flipping Portugal. Many years later Fabrizio will be a wonderful photographer, and his attention to detail makes him a popular nature photographer on Instagram and in real life.

That's how he is. He is also the guy who rings me from Portugal at midnight half-drunk to check if I am okay. But then I bring this wonderful young man to the point.

"Fabry... How is Serena?"

He pauses. I swallow. Not sure I will like what he is about to say.

And then, like in my most secret dreams, he tells me that she isn't behaving as I believe. At all. Against my expectations it isn't the Luca and Serena Love Fest. She actually shares the tent with two of her female friends and doesn't hang around with Luca at all. Not even the day before, when they all slept on the beach by the ocean. It was the first time any of them had ever seen the ocean... And she slept next to her friends!

"Thank you for telling me this, man. I really appreciate it."

"No problem. I thought you'd like to know."

I was happy. I was relieved. In my conflicting emotions, the lust for Signora Vanessa dissipated a little. I felt a bit silly.

Of course Serena was really my destiny and this old woman - in the end - was just nothing. Nothing actually happened, right? She just winked at me for Christ's sake. What was I expecting? What was I dreaming? Of course life will go back to normal as soon as my friends come back from their holidays, and we see each other again.

But then...

"Fabry?"

"Yes..."

"Is she around?"

"Who? Serena? Yes. She's just on the other side of the tent."

"Can you call her, please…"

"Alby…"

"Please…"

"For Christ's sake, why do you always…"

Then a moment of silence and a shout "Serena!"

And a gorgeous familiar voice from far away, "Yes?"

My heart jumps straight into my throat.

There's the sound of a phone being passed over and

"Alberto, on the phone."

Silence. Then a cacophony of whistles, and "Go go go!" Steps getting closer and closer. Laughter in the background. People pretending to sing a wedding song.

"Hello?"

God, is this the sweetest sound in the world?

My mouth is dry. My heart is about to explode. Literally. Again. But a different explosion. Not from the outside in, one deeply entrenched in my being, in my soul.

"You never leave me alone, even here?"

Just before she says anything else, a massive dark thought takes hold of me: how the hell do I justify

Signora Vanessa if I feel this way about Serena? What is wrong with me?

"Sere, don't worry. Goodnight…"

She laughs.

"Joking… Are we a little bit tense? How are you?"

I do not know how to explain it, I just know that Serena is not mine and until I am 100% sure she will be mine I cannot stop the most exciting sensual experience I have ever had.

"How's life in the village? I heard it's very hot."

"Very funny. Yes, it is, since you ask. Very. Who needs the ocean, right?"

"The ocean was amazing yesterday. I'll send you the pic next time I…"

The pause we were both dreading.

"I know I haven't sent you anything for a while. But…"

"Don't worry. You must have your reasons."

"I do. But…"

"But what? "

"I wanted to think about what I feel for you. And for this I needed to not hear from you, to see how much I would miss you."

Man. How can you say these things to an eighteen-year-old boy?

"Do you want to kill me?" (Desperately trying to sound cool but not really succeeding).

"And?"

My heart is in my throat...

"And... I miss you a lot actually."

Breathing again. Huge smile on my face. I close my eyes and raise my hand to the sky, almost dropping the phone, in the gesture of the most incredible number 10 footballer playing for Italy and scoring the decisive penalty against France.

Somebody faraway shouts to her.

"C'mon, are you done with that call? We're here to have fun, okay?"

"Okay, okay. Alby, got to go."

"Okay. Big kiss."

"Big kiss to you too."

"Where?"

"Where what?"

"Where do you want to give me that big kiss?"

"On your... forehead."

"Thanks. Way too sexy."

"Alby?"

"Yes?"

"Tonight, I'm going to dream about you, okay?"

"You dream about me, okay? You promise?"

"Promise."

"Okay. Goodnight then."

"Good..."

Click.

The line goes dead, but the stars couldn't spin any faster. The sky couldn't look more friendly. That night I go to bed with a totally pathetic smile on my face.

Even my dad notices, while still lost in the political issues of the world.

But I don't care.

I go to bed. Serena, Serena, Serena.

I dream about her as instructed. I dream about her as if Signora Vanessa had never existed. Yet somehow knowing that she will reappear at some point. Sooner rather than later. And from somewhere in my mind the idea that maybe I should try not to see the other woman again creeps in.

Just as the dream about Serena becomes more vivid than ever.

CHAPTER 18 - That day I don't go to buy bread. Nor the day after

I say I have to study and lock myself in my room playing video games. I start The Pillars of the Earth, a book by Ken Follett set in the Middle Ages that is eleven hundred pages long. The one that Serena gave me after she stopped reading it at page 23 because there was a scene that upset her.

I reach that scene within a few minutes, and it is a very sexualised scene of betrayal. She got upset about that. Like any good seventeen-year-old she believes in love that lasts forever. She hates cheaters. I have to live up to that, and I have actually never cheated in my whole life. In fact, I couldn't have even if I wanted to - simply because I have never had a proper relationship lasting more than one week until now. So, I don't actually know what cheating means.

All I know today is that I have a good feeling with Serena, and I don't want to spoil it by going up the road and seeing that older woman again. I know that I will feel powerless and probably do something stupid. Or the other half of me says, it is totally irrelevant because that woman, a mature, obviously married yet overtly sensual and sexy woman, doesn't even know you exist, you fool! So just lead your life, relax and do whatever you like.

This second version is developing in my mind.

What if I dreamt it all? I made it all up. All that woman actually did was to wink at me for one second. Is that all? Is this the reason why I'm not leaving home this summer? However, the question is, why did she wink at me? Is it just a game for her? Am I just a game? Well, if I am... shall we play?

No, no, no. I can't play. I've just had the most amazing phone call ever from the girl I love. I can't play. Can I?

Can I? Shall we play then?

I stop reading and go downstairs. The Vespa parked in the garage next to the Panda starts. The small engine sputters in the sweaty summer air, a little wind in my face is sheer delight. Pongo waits by the gate with the leash in his mouth, eager for another one of our runs. I can't do it today, my dear friend. Please understand. When I leave him at home, he barks at me: "Why don't you take me with you?" Sorry, Pongo. Not today.

I reach the top of the road in a few seconds, still smiling. At the traffic light there's a totally deserted feeling. Half of the village is already on holiday. The other half stays inside because of the intense heat.

Green light. My heart starts beating. If I go left that's towards Signora Vanessa's house. I stall. What shall I do? My heart beats faster. I don't move. Amber light turning to red soon. I stare at the light and, just before it turns red, I turn right and head towards the lakes, in the opposite direction, away from her.

I smile at my decisiveness and intention of running away from danger, but the smile is wiped off my face a few seconds later as I run the curve away from the shopping area and there she is, walking back home in sunglasses and an orange dress with a slit so deep that with a little bit of wind it will show her tonsils.

I pretend not to see her and drive straight past as if I were going somewhere in particular. Then I check the rear mirrors to see if she's looking at me. She isn't, and keeps walking as if I hadn't driven past. My heart is in my throat at this precise moment, and she becomes smaller and smaller in my mirror.

Memories of Serena saying she will dream of me whirl through my mind. "Go!" they say. I accelerate towards the lakes. Don't turn around. Drive off as if this were all a distant dream. Or a nightmare. Think about the end of the holidays. Serena will come back, and you will end up being a couple. You are not even going to remember this old woman.

I immediately stop the motorbike. Take a deep breath and turn around.

I go past her again and wave, and she waves back. She keeps on walking, by now fully aware I am circling her like a bird of prey. But who is the prey? Her or me?

I stop again, turn around again and stop next to a small square, by the turning that leads to the school, right in the middle of the village. For the first time the madness of what I am doing hits me. Somebody I know could appear at any time and see me chatting up a married woman. This is Italy in the '80s after all.

My uncle. My cousin. Any of my friends. Their parents. What would they think? An eighteen-year-old boy talking to a skimpily dressed married woman who clearly likes attention. So, what I am going to do? I should just start the Vespa again and ride off. Of course, I should. Right now. Before it's too late.

But of course I stay.

She soars, getting closer and closer on her black heels, one swaying step at a time. By now however I see a smile. I can tell that she is happy to see me, but a bit concerned about gossip herself from the way she looks around. I notice that she has cut her hair. She looks absolutely gorgeous. Objectively.

"Waiting for me?" she breaks the ice.

"Not at all. Just taking a break from a motorbike trip and you went by."

Me trying to be cool and failing miserably, as always.

She lowers her sunglasses and stares at me with her green eyes.

"I saw you going in the opposite direction ten minutes ago."

So, she did notice.

"Well, yes." Bit embarrassing, I guess. "But yes, I wanted to say hi to you. Didn't want to be rude."

"Oh, I see. Well, hi then. Hope to see you at the bakery again."

"Really?"

"Well yes. I missed you. I have to go to the bank now, but... well... let's hope we see each other soon."

What?

She puts her shades back on and starts walking towards the bank.

"Did you?"

A really intense moment...

"Maybe. Have a nice day."

She walks off. Without another word. With that incredible way of walking. All my best intentions are forgotten in a flash. Totally lost in this whirlwind that I cannot explain and that I don't know how to deal with.

"Signora Vanessa?"

She turns around almost in slow motion just as the manager of the local branch, Bruno Bianco, lets her in with a big smile.

"Signora DeLaurentis... What a pleasure..."

"Signor Bianco. Loads of operations to do today. But will you give me a second?"

The bank manager looks at me patronisingly. He is made to wait because of such an insignificant boy? He huffs and puffs and goes back inside.

Signora Vanessa looks back at me. I feel like the most important person in the world.

"Yes?"

"I love your new hairstyle. It really suits you."

"Thank you. A domani."

And against all my wildest expectations she blows me a kiss. It flies through the air gently and hits me in the face like a hammer as she disappears inside the bank. I've really lost my mind. Haven't I?

CHAPTER 19 - That night I went to the cinema by myself to forget the kiss

I had never been to the cinema by myself until just recently. But that evening I HAD to go out and do something. It was hot. It was another sweaty, calm evening. Batman was on at the Borgonuovo Cinema. My father offered to take me by car, but I wanted to go by myself and on my Vespa. The cinema is not far, after all.

I ride off, past Serena's house with all the windows dark as no one is at home and ride further away, towards the block of flats where Signora Vanessa lives.

And of course she is on the balcony wearing a tight pair of hot pants and a tight t-shirt with a very generous neckline. She clearly recognises me, and, as I get closer and closer, I am about to raise my arm to say hello when a man joins her on the balcony. He is much bigger than she is. He has a beard. He is a grown man, who would easily beat the hell out of me in a fight.

My arm stays down but she waves at me. I pretend only now to see her and wave a demure greeting, pretending she doesn't enliven every single moment of my days and nights. Pretending she is nobody, the mother of one of my friends whom I barely know exists, as opposed to the object of all my deepest sensual fantasies.

The man looks away from me and goes back in - clearly unthreatened by a little boy on a blue Vespa. She follows him inside and for the first time I feel jealous.

Who is this big, rough-looking man who enjoys the company of this woman without any limits? Yet... my brain starts wheezing with teenage enthusiasm, naivety and angst.

If this man is so amazing, tough and strong... why is she winking at me, telling me 'See you tomorrow' and, most relevantly, blowing me kisses at their door. Are they kissing now? Are they making love? Is he still making love to her? Maybe he is tired of her after all these years together. Who knows? Maybe he is fed up with a woman who generates (and perhaps craves) so much attention?

Surely it is not all good. Surely, she is not happy, surely now she is thinking of me at least a little bit. Maybe she wants something from me this big man can't give her. What can I give her?

I stop the motorbike again – I look at the time on my Scuba swatch. The film is in thirty minutes. I need to get a confirmation. If I turn around and she comes out on the balcony again she is thinking of me. If she doesn't, she doesn't. It makes perfect sense to me. Right. Let's do it.

I know, please, don't laugh at me!!! I was that sad.

Again, if I turn around and she comes out on the balcony again she is thinking of me. If she doesn't, she doesn't. I turn the motorbike suddenly, causing a car to swerve and curse me. I don't care.

I turn around staring at that balcony. There is no one on the balcony.

Please come out. Please come out. Please come out.

She doesn't.

I turn around again. Heading towards the cinema again.

Please come out.

She doesn't.

I try once more.

She doesn't.

I honk the horn a couple of times.

She doesn't come out.

At that stage I head for the cinema, my morale under my heels, and I arrive as the film is starting. They barely let me in, and thank God it is three hours long. One of the best films ever made by Tim Burton. I loved every second of it and for three hours I forget everything.

Until I ride back, and I see that balcony again. I honk again and I feel a shadow moving in the darkness of the second-floor windows.

I imagine her in bed with her big husband enjoying her and her incredible body and the whole thought makes me sick.

I arrive home, ignore Pongo and my family and lock myself in my bedroom. Thinking about what I should do tomorrow not to go mad.

My father comes in and asks me if everything is ok.

I wish I could say something to him, but he wouldn't understand. He would be disappointed by me chasing a married woman in her forties. That's not what boys like me do right?

So, I smile politely. I go and give him a hug and kiss and tell him I am going to bed. I decline his invitation to go and watch some replay of a football match.

My father gives up and goes back to the kitchen to watch by himself without another word. My mother is already in bed - the lights are off. No reading tonight. I feel guilty so I join him in the kitchen and watch for a little while just to keep him company.

He casually turns to the late-night soft porn program, Drive In, full of comedians and hourglass shaped women in skimpy costumes that become the sex dream of half a generation of Italians. I look at them dancing in the TV studio around the strictly male comedians, and I am surprised that my very serious dad does not change channel within a few seconds. He and I keep looking, pretending that the bad taste, cheap show is not on. An all-male understanding that we shouldn't be watching this, but we are watching it anyway.

After the last bit of the program and the last all female go-go dance, Drive In ends. The screen goes black and the boring, irritating theme song for the end of program starts to play. A few seconds later my father goes to bed.

I stay up a bit longer by myself and then go to bed too. I cover my face with the pillow and start sweating in the sweltering heat, with confused dreams where women from Drive In overlap with Signora Vanessa and, inexplicably, with Serena.

What is happening to me?

CHAPTER 20 - In my dreams

I should think non-stop about Serena who has declared her love for me - or as close as she has ever done in the last three years - but all I can think of is holding Signora Vanessa in my arms. I want to see that incredible body naked. I want her to feel my youthful enthusiasm and energy. God forbid what that experienced woman will do to me. I can already see the Kingdom of Senses, a Fellini-style orgy of depravity, sin and lust.

Yet at the same time in my dreams, I can also see Serena. Looking at me disapprovingly as I make love passionately to a woman only a little bit younger than my mother.

Serena looks at me disappointed. She tells me that she thought I really only loved her, and that no one would love her the way I do, but she was wrong. She was let down by her divorced parents. I shouldn't let her down too.

She shouts at me that I am a fake. I don't really love her. Or at least I don't really lust after her enough. So, she will go and fuck Luca. As she should have done a long time ago. I tell her NO.

I scream it louder and louder. No. No! Noooo!!!

In that moment I wake up in a pool of sweat. It's hot, but it is even hotter in my body and in my heart. I couldn't even begin to imagine this just a few months ago. And I don't like it.

CHAPTER 21 - The Benches. Empty

It is very strange to go to a place that is normally buzzing with people and be alone there.

I arrive at the Benches with my Vespa, and it is so, so, so strange to be by myself. It is incredible to notice for the first time in my life how places that you love so much become totally pointless when there is no one to share emotions with. The Benches at the park without my friends now travelling around Europe become like an empty family home: bare, meaningless walls full of past memories that resonate only in the mind. I even brought my basketball, but I can't bring myself to play for more than ten minutes. I sit on a bench and start reading the graffiti.

All the people I miss so much. Claudio. Fabrizio. Serena. Giorgio. Andrea. Even the people I couldn't stand. Giuseppe. Bettori. Colla. All those idiots.

The sun is shining. The village is all mine, but I have no idea what I can do with it.

So, I start riding up and down the two kilometres of main road, up and down from the pond at one end of the village to the little hill at the other end. From the tennis courts at one end to the mega estate of the millionaire family from Geneva on the other side. It's hot, even driving up and down in the wind on the Vespa, helmet fully open.

It is late in the afternoon and there is virtually no one in the street. I will run out of petrol soon if I carry on like this.

She works from home so I think she will be there, but her husband won't be back from work yet. Then, just like in a dream she comes out, onto the balcony. I ride past and wave. She waves back. I stop the motorbike and look back. She is still on the balcony.

So, on the spur of the moment, not really knowing what I am doing, I turn around. Go back. She watches me as I park by her door. I see a few bells, pick the one with her surname and ring it hard.

She answers after a few seconds.

"Yes?"

"Sono Alberto."

"No. I have people coming soon"

"Not even five minutes?"

"No. Tomorrow."

CLICK

I go back to a long, lonely night and the cinema. When I leave home my mother repeats the old cliché that 'this house is not a hotel,' etc. My father shakes his head and tells her to let me do whatever I like. Grazie Papa.

The guy at the cinema box office clearly thinks I have an addiction. They have two screens and I have already seen both films.

They now have a special summer program showing a different film every night at a reduced price or, for a special price, one can watch all the films that summer.

It is that special ticket that keeps me going in the evenings.

But the nights are long.

CHAPTER 22 - And of course the day after I get a card

The next day I get a card. It is from London, my favourite place. The city I've always wanted to visit. The place that sounds so cool. The place where I have no inkling at the moment that I will spend the rest of my life. Fabrizio is there now and will bring me home a leaflet from the London film school - the school that in a few years will change my life.

The postcard shows Piccadilly Circus with its iconic screens. I flip the card and I read Serena's tidy writing. Written very small from the beginning. She wanted to tell me a lot. I refuse to read it at home. I put the card under my shirt, and I ride off - and where else could I go in an empty village other than at the Benches.

No one around. Just me and my Vespa. I park by our usual bench and sit in the corner where I wrote her name in permanent marker. Only then do I take out her postcard.

The card reads:

> "Ciao Alby. Come va? I hope all good. Here is great but I miss you really a lot. I have no idea what to think and what to feel. I understand if you are angry with me, but at the same time I hope you can understand. I am just confused. More confused than ever. At night I wonder and think about

you, but during the day we travel, we laugh, we enjoy ourselves and I feel I am happy as I am, and I don't want to be anybody's girlfriend. I don't know if you can understand. I want to be with you. I want to be close to you, but I am only seventeen, Alby. I don't know if I am ready to be in a full-on relationship, especially with someone as important as you, Alby. I know no one will ever love me like you do, but I am not ready for that love maybe.

Ti voglio bene. Sere xxx"

This is what my eighteen-year-old heart doesn't understand.

This is a black hole. There are emotions that I can't understand yet. How is it possible to be in love with someone and not want their love? There are a lot of things I don't know yet, but I do know that I want to be with Serena forever. I want her to be my girlfriend. I want to be with her. She doesn't want to be with me. We go around in circles and there is just so much we can take.

But this summer is changing me in a way that I wouldn't expect.

I know and you know that to fight this pain I will chase Signora Vanessa again for the comfort of the excitement. Something to make me forget my heartache and give me back my confidence

I will go and ring her bell.

She will let me in, and I will climb those stairs two by two.

I will open the door of her apartment and she will start kissing me before I even get inside, and I will make love to her like a stallion. Again, and again.

Then I will leave satisfied, but in the same situation.

Why can't I be in London? Why can't I be with Serena? How long is this torture going to last? Most importantly: will I ever manage to be with her? Will I ever be happy?

This and a million other questions whirl in my head until I lift my eyes.

I see the light.

I ride to Signora Vanessa's home. Ring the bell. No answer. Try again. No answer.

She is not home.

I go home and wait for the news. Please, God, make sure something has happened in the world or tonight I just couldn't take it. Thank God, something happens.

CHAPTER 23 - My wonderful dad-Part 2

It is tonight that the special bond between me and my amazing, gorgeous, innocent father develops into one of the most important relationships in my life. We talk about politics. He tells me of the importance for him, someone who believes in Communism as a force for good, as a political drive that has brought us where we are, that someone like me, the son of a lowly engineer, could have a virtually free education, and one day hope to go to university – the first person in my family to do so. But I just couldn't take it.

I listen to my father's comments on this strike in Eastern Europe and what it means for workers like him. Who fought for their rights to be respected. And yet my father doesn't know that I'm thinking something totally different. And frankly, tonight I couldn't care less about the workers in Siberia.

But tonight, I need company, Papa. I can't be alone - and all my friends are gone. I don't know what to do, Papa, and I wish very much I could talk to you about how my heart is split between senses and loyalty - between light and darkness. I want to choose the light, Papa, but my body is taking me towards the excitement of darkness.

A man and a boy, sitting next to each other on the sofa, each talking a language the other doesn't understand.

I rest my head on his big shoulders, tempered by years of hard, physical labor. I am sure my dad could defend me from Signora Vanessa's husband if I were caught in her bed. But would he be proud of me and my behaviour?

My father is still going on about the workers in Siberia, but realises I am not listening to a single word. He stops.

"You couldn't care less about the workers in Siberia, could you?"

A pause.

"No, Papa."

"Are you thinking about a girl?"

This old man knows me so well.

"Two."

"Ah. Choose well."

And this simple, wonderful, straight man of few words kisses me on the forehead and disappears to sleep the sleep of the just. And his wavering, quivering wreck of a son stays up, less sure than ever of what to do with his life.

CHAPTER 24 - NO. The longest two letters in the world

Prisons of the body and the mind are called first world problems. When you are in a nice home, in a nice village, in a prosperous part of Italy, but you are miserable. Why? Because your girlfriend (or actually the girl you would love to be your girlfriend) is on a trip with someone else in Europe. This is my biggest problem. And it is not a real problem - yet this summer THIS is my prison. I live in my own personal prison every time Signora Vanessa says no to me that summer.

I go and buy bread again. She is nowhere to be seen.

I ring her bell.

"No. Come back tomorrow."

Tomorrow. Another long day and night.

I go and buy bread again. God, how much more bread do I need to buy???

She comes out and walks though the empty streets looking amazing. How long does it take her every morning to look like this? Again. When she sees me, I feel she looks at me like she never did before. Today she has an orange blouse with three buttons open, offering an unrivalled view. I feel today is my lucky day, so I switch off my Vespa and I push it along, walking alongside her... and she lets me.

We talk side by side on her way back home, chatting like two old friends about the weather, and about how the whole village is empty now. Anything really. She asks about my studies, and I tell her that all my friends are travelling through Europe in this very momentous year - when everything is changing on a daily basis. She smiles with a hint of bitterness.

"Only in this village things never change, do they? Maybe we should run away together, Alberto? And see a bit of the world, away from our TV screens?"

I smile back and walk slowly, pushing my motorbike all the way to her home, wishing this conversation would never end.

"What would you like to see?"

"Australia - she says - I want to see the other side of the world. It's always been my dream. A long, long trip to Australia. I want to swim in their sea and enjoy everything the country has to offer... and then after that MAYBE come back."

That I did not expect.

"Don't you think there are too many dangerous animals? "

"Don't be such a wimp. Think about swimming in those wonderful seas. It might be life changing. I really don't know if I would ever come back."

I dream of a sea of crystalline water, but the end is nigh. The road from the shops to her house is not long. Before I can park my bike, she is inside her gate, waving goodbye from the other side of the glass front door.

I gesture for her to let me in.

"I can't," she says and blows me a kiss before disappearing up the stairs.

Before I can do anything else, her neighbour comes down. She is probably same age as Signora Vanessa, but looks like her mother - all frumpy cardigans and a shapeless grey skirt. She looks at me severely with a sharp 'Buongiorno', making sure she has shut the door before I can even think about going in.

The severe neighbour takes a few steps and then comes back and actually checks who I am.

"Do you actually need anything?"

"No, signora. Just waiting for my friend."

"And who is your friend?"

God, this woman. Can't she just mind her own business? Quick panic. Whom do I know in the same block of flats? One guy. Giorgio Diamante. Is this woman going to spread rumors about me? Is this the last time I can come here?

"Giorgio Diamante."

The nosy neighbour relaxes and even smiles for the first time.

"Look, the Diamante family lives next door, and the gate is actually the one over there."

"Oh, I see" - praying that Giorgio Diamante doesn't come down the stairs right now and make me look like a stalker.

"I'll go and wait for him there now."

The nosy busybody walks off eventually, reassured. I am off the hook.

Signora Vanessa is up on her balcony already in shorts and a revealing t-shirt, ready to populate my dreams again.

I look up. She smiles and says coquettishly "Careful with that motorbike." Just what she said that first day.

I should be careful of YOU, I feel like screaming. But I don't. I just smile, nod and head back home before the inquisitive neighbour returns.

"I give up," I say before turning on my bike.

"Don't," she says again.

I stop. I look up, not sure I heard properly.

"Erm... Excuse me?" I say VERY hesitantly.

"You must NEVER give up on something that you really, really want. Very important lesson in life."

She smiles, and walks back inside with that strutting walk of hers. I just stand there.

After dinner, my mother is tired and goes to bed early, so my father and I end up watching that TV show again, full of showgirls in pretty much the same dresses with the same curves as Signora Vanessa. My father watches disapprovingly, mumbling about watching something more cultural, forgetting he was watching exactly the same show a few days earlier.

But as soon as we hear my mother snoring, we watch together. It is our secret, and we want to keep it that way. I wish I only had that secret to keep. I have too many secrets that I don't want to keep anymore, and I need a way out of this.

CHAPTER 25 - YES, but not in the way you might expect

I think there is something about me and people saying no.

I just burn with an incredible determination and stubbornness to prove them wrong. I feel my dogged courtship of Serena, especially in the face of her silence from her European trip, is part of that. I don't know if it is really love or just the crazy determination to prove her wrong, to show that I am stronger than she is. Even if this sometimes (in fact quite often) sends me in the wrong direction.

I have never experienced anyone like Signora Vanessa outside wet dreams in front of MAGGIORATE of Drive In.

I think those women have ruined - or spiced up - my dreams to the point where I feel I HAVE to go upstairs to Signora Vanessa's flat. Doing what I have no idea, but it seems to be yet another challenge I have to accomplish.

So here I am.

I drive up and down the high street, past the only three shops that are still open. Again. I wait for Signora Vanessa to appear looking amazing. She does, and I walk her back home secretly praying the curious neighbour won't come down again.

I wait for her to let me in. She looks at me and, incredibly, says "Give me fifteen minutes."

After checking my watch every few seconds, I ring the bell again at thirteen minutes and thirty-seven seconds later.

"Yes?"

She answers, as though she didn't know I was there.

"It's Alberto, Signora."

The buzzer opens the door. Time stops.

O H M Y G O D!!!

She has actually buzzed the door. Open.

Is this it? Is this what dreams are made of?

I open the door to the hall slowly, finding it hard to believe the coast is clear. Then I have to run out again as in the emotion of the occasion I forgot the keys of my Vespa on the dashboard. No one is going to steal my old scooter, but you never know.

As soon as I am inside, I race up the four flights of stairs jumping four steps at a time. My heart is beating like never before. Not even Serena has ever had this effect on me. My heart is about to burst into flames. I've never felt like this before and won't again for a long time.

144

The scent of her unmistakable perfume is stronger than ever outside her door. I inhale deeply as if it were some incredible drug and realise the door is ajar. So, I go in.

Now the sexed-up teenage beast turns back into the very polite Piemontese boy and, totally oblivious of the fact that I am about to enter the home of a forty-six-year-old married woman in shorts and a tight t-shirt with a plunging neckline. A woman whom I have court-ed incessantly for the last fifteen days (so that half of the village is probably gossiping about it) and whom I have dreamed of fucking senseless for fifteen eternal, sleepless nights; I revert to polite manners - no idea why.

I wipe my shoes on the mat outside her door.

"May I come in?"

"Come on in," she says from the other room, just as casually, as if it were the most normal situation in the world.

As if she hadn't just let a teenager desperate to have sex with her - ideally taking off her clothes within the next ten seconds - into her flat.

As if we didn't know that technically our little liaison would be barely legal and, if my birthday were just a couple of months later, would be classified as sex with a minor, a crime punishable by a jail sentence for her.

None of that mattered.

Face to face and alone at last, we look at each other strangely - the distance is small yet still immense. We both know no one can see us. We are free. Whatever is about to happen will be a secret forever if we want that. Or perhaps nothing will ever happen. I have no idea if her heart is beating as fast as mine but, if it is, she is hiding it pretty well behind the slightly old-fashioned glasses I've never seen her wear before. They immediately make her look slightly older, spoiling her craftily created brand of sex appeal and sophistication.

The flat is nice, and interestingly decorated. She clearly has good taste and perhaps even a bit of money. She is sitting at her round kitchen table, sewing and listening to the business news on TV. That strikes me. She looks at me briefly, checking whether I like what I see before returning to her work. I look at her with eyes full of desire, and just hug her from behind and kiss her neck.

"Don't distract me. I am following the market."

"Buying or selling?"

"Well, the market is going up... quite well. I bet on an American stock and it's making me very, very happy. Maybe I got a winner after all."

She smiles and focuses on her work, but doesn't move my trembling hands. My lips are on her ears now and she moves away gently.

"Slowly, slowly, what is the rush?"

"Ah... You know how long I've had to wait for this?"

"Good things come to those who wait."

Well, I think, apart from the fact that it took me fifteen days to get here, it took me fifteen sleepless nights dreaming what it would be like to be here and now I have you in my arms. But it's not going to be that straightforward, is it?

And of course, I can't say that.

"Are you making money on the market, Signora Vanessa?"

"I make more money in the stock market than making dresses for all these fat housewives and their daughters..."

This woman is not going to just take off her clothes, and I realise I have no idea how to MAKE a woman like this interested in me.

I try to be charming, but it's not easy.

"No woman in the village has your body... but you can't blame them for trying to look like you..."

"Well, I'm making a dress for Serena's mother... She used to be skinnier, but she's let herself go a little bit. Her daughter looks very nice though."

My mind races: the fact that she's let me in her flat makes me wonder if she would like me to take the initiative. Is this how a mature woman responds? Or why let me come up to her flat? But why is she talking about Serena?

Perhaps this is as much a fantasy for her as it is for me?

"Do you like Serena?"

I am eighteen, and I don't have the slightest clue what to say next. I have no idea if she wants me to take off her clothes and perhaps even to kiss her. What she doesn't know but probably suspects by now is that I am still a virgin - I know, please don't laugh. I have seen a female genital organ maybe three times and always on television. I've touched one once. And I have never seen a pair of breasts like hers, exploding beneath her flimsy t-shirt and ballooning up the plunging neckline with the aid of a push-up bra that has no purpose other than creating the most erotic sight I have ever seen.

"Serena is a very nice girl. I have no idea what you are doing here when you could be with her..."

If this was meant to pour cold water on my passion it didn't work. All I could do was to hug, stare and watch for any hint of denial. She remains predictably in control and my hands wander around for a while, but she doesn't react. I am disappointed. This is not what I was expecting.

I feel shattered. Now I REALLY don't know what to do.

But she realises I don't have a clue, stops working and takes off her glasses.

I really don't know what I am doing here and am about to give up when she turns around, stands up and hugs me, both arms around my neck, making damn sure I feel those gigantic breasts on my chest, separated from my body only by a non-existent layer of cotton. She kisses me slowly, then passionately, and I am about to die and go to heaven or…

"Now you have to go."

WHAAAAAAATTTTTTTTTTTTTT?

"You must. You have to go if you want to come back."

I look at her, not really sure what she means. However, I do as she says. Even if I think it doesn't make any sense.

So, I stand up. I kiss her on the lips again - strictly no tongue this time and leave.

Once I'm outside, reality floods back.

I don't know if this is all a dream, if I actually went to her flat, hugged her, touched her, kissed her. I've lost all sense of time. One hour and a half have gone. I can't believe I spent an hour and half in her flat, alone with the woman of my dreams, and yet it felt like only five minutes.

I go down the steps. Slowly, one at a time. I want to savour the moment, whatever that means. It feels like total elation. I'm on top of the world.

As I reach the bottom of the stairs, the door is there, my Vespa is there, and the warm evening breeze embraces me. I don't feel low anymore. I feel up in the sky as I look up at that balcony and see her there. Smiling.

I wave. She waves back.

This clearly feels like a dream, but I know it won't be the last time I go there.

PART 4 – August 1989 - Alone in the village - and trying to stay alive

A brief disquisition about the nature of summer in a small village in the north of Italy from the point of view of someone who has lived in London for twenty years.

If you don't come from Italy, it is very hard to understand the nature of the weeks from the middle of July till the end of August in our psyche and background as a nation. Italy from June onward is VERY hot. I remember the ironic looks of my Northern European friends when everything shutting down in Italy in August was mentioned. They would wear slightly superior smirks and whisper funny little comments about how lazy and inefficient Italians are. That is until they actually CAME to Italy in August. Then no more smirks as understanding came.

Italy in August is HELL unless you are on holiday – Thirty-five-degree heat and dry sunshine for twenty-eight days in a row. Everybody is on holiday. Factories are shut. Shops are shut and everyone moves to the seaside. Nothing is available in the city. People in Italy truly resent being anywhere in August other than by the seaside (or if you come from a radically chic family in the mountains or on a lake). Because that's the flip side: if you are in a lovely place by the seaside, Italy in August can truly be heaven.

Beautiful unspoiled beaches, fantastic scenery, the warm water of the Mediterranean, fantastic food everywhere, more art than you will ever manage to absorb and, if you are a hormonal spotty teenager like me, absolutely jam-packed with girls. Girls at the seaside are heaven. No one knows them. They don't know you. Their clothes are off. Their parents are tired, and what

153

goes on at the seaside... no one back at the village needs to know. Heaven, right?

Yes, it is.

Unless of course you are in a small village in the Northwestern Alps. Alone. All your friends are away, and even the older lady who made your summer bearable goes to see her relatives in Sicily.

Then August does become the longest month of the year. The month when you are so bored that so as not to lose your mind you have to do something creative that doesn't make you sweat. Such as writing. Anything to keep your mind busy when even walking the dog in the countryside becomes torture. In thirty-five degrees, I don't envy Pongo with his luscious grey and white coat. We open the garage for him out of pity. It is just too hard to be an old English sheepdog in Italy. Sometimes, I feel just like him. Alone in an inhospitable and hostile world.

CHAPTER 26 - I have no idea what it must have felt like for a married woman but...

That night as I lie down in bed, I think about what we did (or didn't) do.

I wanted to punch myself for not having tried to do more, achieve more, get more, but I feel warm and fuzzy too. Whatever it was we did, it felt good. Too good. Frighteningly good.

In fact, so good that I have no idea how it could have happened, but it did happen. In a world away I feel, even just for a short while, this incredible woman was MINE. Issue of course is... what does that actually mean? What am I going to do with it? She is thirty years older than me, married and almost as old as my mother. What can we do together anyway... beyond more of what we just did?

But also. What does it mean for me and Serena, the girl I've spent the last three years chasing? Does it mean I am not really in love with Serena because this happened? Does it mean I technically cheated on Serena? But I am SINGLE! Serena told me very clearly a few days ago, very categorically, that she is NOT my girlfriend, much as I sometimes behave as if she is. So, I actually only kissed a married woman, but this doesn't really feel like my own problem. At all. I didn't cheat on anyone and if SHE did... that is what SHE has to worry about. Right?

RIGHT? I don't know. Too much fog in my head.

As I go to sleep, all I can feel is that I want to go to that flat again. I am scared by the strength of these emotions, and I am frightened by how these emotions are making me blank out Serena. I almost feel as if I don't care about Serena any more. But surely that is not possible! That cannot happen now. I love Serena, right? She is the love of my life, but if she is the love of my life why does my heart beat at the thought of going to Signora Vanessa's flat?

I close my eyes and I want the morning to come. Immediately.

I sleep.

Deep sleep. Visions. Us. Serena. Hugs. Kisses. Vanessa. My heart in my throat. Serena again.

It's a long, agitated night. The two women twirl in my dreams and in my imagination. Until the sun comes up and, as I try to sleep, my mother wakes me up at an unusually early hour.

"Alberto…"

Silence. I don't hear anything. It's just a faint sound very far away.

"Albertoooooooo!"

"Who is it?"

"ALBERTOOOOOOO!!!"

My mother has now been shouting at me for five minutes. She's pulled away my sheets. The window is open, and the room is already hot. She looks impatient.

"C'mon..."

"What's up, Mamma? It's summer!!! I don't have to go to school tomorrow!"

"Serena's downstairs..."

It takes me five seconds to realise what she just said. I look at her. Apron on. A demure blue summer dress, ideal to stay fresh in these hot temperatures. Looking at me very annoyed.

"What?"

Did she say what I just heard her say?

"Serena is downstairs. Shall I let her come up?"

"Yes! No. Yes... YES!"

NOOOOOO! WAIT!

I jump in the bath, have a forty-five-second shower, deodorant and gel galore, and grab a coffee as my head is still spinning. No, this is not meant to be happening TODAY. Why today? For God's sake!!!

I feel I have betrayal written all over me, but the thing is... we are not even together. So why do I feel I have cheated on her? She is not even my girlfriend so why do I care so much? And why am I so scared of being 'caught'?

I open the main door and there she is. Serena, playing with Pongo – whom she probably missed more than me.

The window behind her creates a halo of warm light as if a fifteen-day tan and sun-bleached blonde hair were not enough as the dog leaps shamelessly around her. She is just wearing a simple pair of denim shorts and a t-shirt, but I swear to God, cheesy as it sounds, I have never, EVER, seen anyone more beautiful. The eyes, the tan, the blond hair... Oh my God... and well, God... she knows it. This is all so bloody confusing.

"Are you going to close your mouth?"

She always manages...

I shake my head.

"Closed. Happy?"

"Great. It looks like Pongo is happier to see me than you are."

"Thanks. Here I am. Ciao."

She doesn't look convinced.

"Is this all you have to say to me?"

"And what do you want me to say?"

"Something a bit... I don't know. A bit... more? Aren't you happy to see me?"

She looks at Pongo.

"Pongo, can you tell Alberto how to welcome me a little more warmly? Just like you do."

She looks at me more intently.

"A girl who, after three weeks spent in Europe, the first thing that she does... she comes to your house, and you welcome her like this? But maybe if it's the wrong moment I'll go and call on someone else..."

I grab her hand as she makes a pretend walking away gesture.

"Thank you. Come here."

"You're welcome. With a present."

I admit something inside of me is dying. The last broken pieces of conscience, of a soul turning on itself. What the fuck am I doing? Who am I?

"Do you want to see your present?"

"Sure."

She sits down on the bed next to me and hands me a beautifully wrapped box. She's always had this knack for giving very good presents. I unwrap the ribbon and the paper, and inside the paper box are... just a few pieces of brick and cement.

I look at her unsure what this means. She smiles sarcastically.

"You don't get it, do you?" she asks...

I'm lost...

"No..."

She looks up to the sky, then at me - as if I were a total retard...

"Where did I go?"

"Everywhere in bloody Europe actually... as far as I know..."

I look at the box with all her postcards next to my bed...

"I have the proof..."

She looks at the postcards she wrote a few days before. So much has happened, so much has changed.

"It's as if someone else wrote them..."

"Really..."

Another long pause.

"Yes. But... where was the magical place that we always wanted to go - in this incredibly mad summer of '89?"

"Berlin?"

"Yes."

"The Wall."

"The Wall. That is exactly what it is. It's a piece of the Wall. The Berlin Wall. It was so exciting. I wish you had been there. I just developed the photos, but I don't have them yet. Should have them by tomorrow. It was mad. People everywhere. The guards look at them and don't do anything. If they had done something like this six months ago, they would have been shot. But not now. The guards look at them peacefully. Some of the people on top of the Wall were throwing flowers at the guards. It was crazy.

"And this is a piece of THAT wall?"

"It is. It is a testament that everything is possible, Alby. If the Berlin Wall falls after forty years... the world can change, and I keep my promises..."

"So maybe even you and me can be together - after all?"

"After all. As long as the Wall falls."

"And will it?"

She shrugs. "No one knows for sure."

I hold this historical piece of brick in my hands. I feel an extraordinary energy.

Something special happens between us. We look at each other with different eyes. We hug again. We kiss, briefly. Her lips always felt sooo soft.

She looks up from the hug and it just makes my life easier.

"Listen. I have three days here, and then I have to go on holiday with my mum for another month. Let's not waste a minute of it. What do you say?"

"I say, let's go for a ride on a Vespa?"

"Now you're talking. You know, I have to leave the day after tomorrow?"

"Plenty of time."

"And I won't be back for another month."

"You told me. I'll survive."

"With Pongo?"

Pongo looks up expectantly - wiggling his massive derriere as fast as he can.

"No, Pongo."

Then she looks at me with those beautiful blue eyes that I used to dream about every night until fifteen days ago and says: "I was dying to see you."

I freeze.

I am not sure what that means. I have been waiting for this for so long, and now that it is right here in front of me, I don't know what to do with it.

Serena feels it and doesn't hesitate. Her lips, pink from lip-gloss, come closer. I caress her gorgeous blonde hair, like I've always wanted to do. Her arm, tanned and toned from three weeks around Europe, pulls me towards her and we kiss again, and the most amazing twenty-four hours ever begin - exactly the opposite to what I expected the day before.

But I can't help making a goofy comment: "Sere... Can I show the Berlin Wall piece to my dad? You know all the Communist party regalia stuff... he'll love it."

She smiles.

"Sure. Maybe after that your dad will hate me a bit less."

"He doesn't hate you. He just thinks that your dad is full of shit... but only because he drives a Ferrari, which is an un-Communist thing to do."

"He worked very hard for it..."

"Drop it, shall we? Papaaaaaaaaaaaa?"

163

From the other room: "What is it?"

"Can I show you a piece of the Berlin Wall?????"

My father looks at the bricks... a bit startled.

"Where did you get it?"

"Serena got it in Berlin."

My father looks at it again.

"I don't know if I should laugh or cry..."

"Very much the same feeling I have."

CHAPTER 27- Disappearing together

What happens next is wrapped in the velvet of a somewhat old-fashioned jazz song, one of those songs that works so well at night, when the only source of light is a candle.

Serena and I just disappear from our own lives and from our present. We tell our parents we will be back tonight and just leave. Both sets of parents nod knowingly - fully aware nothing can stop us today.

The old piece of the Berlin Wall is left behind with my father, who decides it should be encased in a specially made glass container and has already started to draw up plans and buy materials.

My traditional adoring mother starts making sandwiches for us almost immediately. Serena's younger and cooler mother just gives her a stupid amount of money to spend on God knows what. As if we were going to the end of the world.

Both our parents must have seen our names scribbled on a million pages of our diaries next to hearts, just to be deleted and scribbled over two seconds later. Enough to understand that arguing with us about our plans for today would be futile. We are young and in love. We cannot disappear to Bali, but we can disappear on my Vespa towards the mountains, looking for the perfect spot to have the longest conversations in our lives.

Up and down the hills around our village, in green forests surrounded by mountains that even in summer still have their snowcap, we ride and ride, laugh and laugh, our souls singing in unison and our bodies feeling comfortable with one another.

We ride. We talk. We kiss. We do all the things we said we would do while we were away from one another. We eat freshly made sandwiches in a field above the lake. We drink water from a stream. We run and chase each other through a field full of lavender flowers. We eat gelato in the empty town square kissed by the sun. We kiss again. It is a different kiss from Signora Vanessa. This kiss is soft, glowing, perfect. This is a kiss on top of MONTERUNI, the little hill with the view of the twin lakes below, our local attraction. Our secret place. The place where we went out together for the first time. The place where we first kissed all those years ago.

Kissing on top of Monteruni, while looking at the reflection of the sun in the twin lakes below, makes us feel like a proper couple, like an accomplished fact, two people who are eventually happening. As if it was always destiny.

No need to say we also talk about her trip across Europe - meant to be the worst nightmare of my life. And yet somehow it wasn't. But I knew this conversation was coming. She wants to tell me what happened on that trip, and I am not quite sure I want to know. How it was, the million feelings that she always wanted to experience. What it was like in Paris. Berlin. London. Like she always wanted to know - experience all the place -

and in my mind I can't repeat... Yes, you experienced all of this WITHOUT ME. And it doesn't feel right.

Why she said what she said when she was in London and how she changed her mind. The incredible people that she met, from the Korean girls on a train to Malaga to the guys playing guitar at the Sacré Coeur in Paris, and the Iranian boy who sang Purple Rain in a dodgy wine bar near Old Compton Street in London. And in the middle of this she tells me how fast her heart was beating when she knew she was coming to see me again. So, it is as if the Interrail, the last three weeks, never happened, for her or for me.

I have to stop for a second as I listen to her. This girl, my girl, sounds just like a girl totally in love, who wants to let me know she is in love with me now, after I have been chasing her for three years. Now she is telling me everything I always wanted her to tell me, yet, as she talks, whispering in my ear as we ride the Vespa up and down the hills around our village, I am afraid that behind my Ray Ban sunglasses, I'm looking somewhere else.

Serena is telling me everything I always dreamt of, yet as we get closer and closer to our village on the Vespa, and stroll in those gentle hills, I find myself longing to have a look at Signora Vanessa's balcony. This is a total shock to my system and to my body - but a huge hit on my soul. Serena doesn't even notice as she rests her head on my shoulders, but my heart has almost shut down.

I can't believe I am feeling like this with Serena behind me, hugging me tight, for once showing me how she really feels. But I can't stop myself - and I don't actually know why. It would be so easy to let myself accept all this pure love - but I can't.

Then, out of the blue, she says "You know, Alberto, I'm not sure if we can be together though..."

And it is at this sentence, spoken exactly then and there, that all my dented confidence just drains away.

As I ride past the shops and the bakery, Serena keeps talking and breathing in my ear, but my mind is elsewhere. I realise I am distracted, and my heart starts beating faster... but not because of what she is saying.

"I don't know if you can wait for me until the end of the summer holidays, but when I come back from the South of Italy, I do hope we can be together. Can you wait until then?"

Against my will, I look up at THE OTHER WOMAN'S balcony. I don't do it on purpose. I didn't even expect to. It just happened. Serena doesn't even notice. She is too busy pouring her heart out. I smile, she smiles back. She thinks I'm smiling at her. She kisses me on my lips, but my heart sinks and I feel like a traitor - even if it is Serena who just rejected me - yet again.

And somehow... it happens. I freeze. Serena keeps on going for a little while longer before she notices my silence.
She asks if everything is ok, but her mood stays jubilant. It would take very little effort to pretend everything is ok and let her leave the day after tomorrow with her

heart full of happiness and hope that in September we will eventually end up being a couple.

But I just cannot fake it.

I am totally frozen and disconnected.

She doesn't understand what is going on yet, but I feel I need to take her home. She doesn't understand why I don't say a word. It would take so little effort to patch it up, to make it up, to start kissing again - even if she does want her freedom to do whatever she wants in Southern Italy. But I can't. She doesn't need to go home yet. But I think I need some time to think, to breathe, to process everything that is happening to me.

The Vespa slowly turns around and heads towards our road, her house. I'm not looking at her, but I can feel her body slacken when she realises, I am taking her home, that our magic day is not coming to the perfect end she may have wanted.

"What's up?" she eventually explodes.

"Nothing." And we both know it's a lie.

"Nothing?"

"Nothing."

"And you have nothing else to say? I've been speaking for an hour, and we've gone up and down the hills all day, and now you don't say a word. But you tell me it's nothing."

"It's nothing. Go to Southern Italy, have fun and let's meet up again when you come back."

We ride the Vespa all the way back to her house in a chilly silence. It must have been thirty-two degrees, but we are both shivering from the frost that suddenly separates us.

I don't know why I feel the overwhelming need to destroy her almost perfect dream.

As she gets off the Vespa, she looks at me as if something has been broken - maybe forever.

"You know I have to leave the day after tomorrow."

"You've told me that a million times."

"And I won't be back for another month."

"You've told me that a million times too... and you've also told me a million times that you are not sure about us... especially when you are about to go on holiday in Southern Italy... maybe there is someone there waiting for you..."

"What are you talking about?"

"I don't know, Serena. I don't know how I feel..."

"You know, when I was in Berlin, I really felt that everything can change. Everything can happen. If the Berlin Wall can fall, then everything in life can happen."

"Just as the world changes, we realise that not EVE-RYTHING can change..."

"Why are you trying to sound so cynical? This doesn't sound like you. I know you are better than this? Don't be like this. You know, Alberto, I always feel you like to be washed away by the current, but sometimes in life you have to take a stand. You have to fight for things to work."

"Tell yourself that, Serena... it can't always be about me fighting for you. Sometimes you have to fight yourself, you know. Will you ever be ready to fight for me? I doubt it..."

This hurts. I regret saying it the minute the words come out of my mouth, but they're out now.

She opens her garden gate in a rush, and before I can say anything she slams it shut and runs inside crying.

Her mother appears at the door and Serena goes in without a word, tears still in her eyes. The stern looks her mother gives me says it all. Here is her beautiful teenage daughter back from a life-changing trip across Europe and within a few hours the local scumbag reduces her to tears.

She darts me a look full of hatred and doesn't even say goodbye. She turns around theatrically and shuts the door.

I remain in front of her gate for a few more seconds, not really sure how I could have messed up something that was so clearly going to be perfect, and manage to destroy it all in a few hours. Admittedly with a lot of help from Serena herself.

I can see the doorbell in front of me. Her surname is written in neat red lettering in a conservative font. A little grey button of plastic, and I could ring the bell and go inside, reverse it all, stop it all. Beg her to forgive me. She didn't know what I was thinking after all. I can even use the excuse of being jealous of her and Luca. Perfect way back in. How it was just a moment of madness and can we start all over again.

But I don't. I go home. Pongo sees me coming back, but he doesn't even bother to get up. Before I go to sleep, I cry in the quiet darkness of my room.

My dad pops his head in. He asks me if I want to watch television. I say no.

If he can detect the tears, he doesn't say anything. This is not what men do. Especially not men of his generation. He comes to give me a kiss on the forehead and goes back to the television. Alone.

Somehow when he leaves, after a few seconds I feel an impossible urge, so I stand up, walk to the kitchen and lie on the sofa in front of the television set, next to my father's legs, my head resting on his belly.

We don't say another word. That's all we both need. And we know it. It is there, away from eyes that could see any weakness in my indestructible father, he caresses my hair gently. It is just wonderful. Just what I need at this moment. Tomorrow is another day.

My father comes into my room and switches on the bedside lamp. He shows me what he's been doing the whole day: the little piece of the Berlin Wall is now resting on a wooden base and protected by a plexiglass casing. He has even sculpted a little label that reads 'Berlin Wall - 1989'.

It looks very, very nice, and my father leaves it by my side, next to the books. He gives me a kiss and goes to bed.

CHAPTER 28 - How would you help me?

The next day the sun shines again, as always. The mountains haven't moved, and the earth is still spinning around. Breakfast is plentiful and delicious, and the radio plays the old-fashioned songs my mother enjoys so much. She sings along and I go to give her a kiss. She is the most out-of-tune person in the world, but hearing her sing always makes me smile. I feel I don't even know what I did yesterday – and this is just another day of reading pointless books and waiting for my life to restart. September can't arrive soon enough.

As I read upside-down on my bed, my dad comes into the room and asks: "Do you want to earn a bit of money?"

I look at him. This is a man who worked HARD. This is a man who walked back home from GERMANY after the end of the Second World War. A man who has known struggle and because of that a man who never wanted his only child to ever suffer the physical pain he went through. He never EVER wanted me to work as he felt it reflected badly on him. He can AFFORD for his son not to have to work. That's how I became the spoilt brat that I have turned into. But maybe the good times are about to end.

"Sure. What do I have to do?"

"Help Raffaello with a house as an electrician."

"As an electrician, Papa? I do business studies. I have no idea what an electrician does."

"Don't worry. That's what Raffaello is for. He'll explain"

"Ok."

"So I tell him, ok? Don't you want to know the pay?"

"Ahem... sure."

My intense fascination with deals and negotiating is already very apparent.

"Sixty thousand lira a day."

"Wow. That's a lot of money."

At that time, you could buy a car for 1.2 m lira.

"And why is he paying me so well?"

"Well, apparently that's the going rate. So, you see, if you decide not to study for another year, there's another well-paid job waiting for you."

"Don't worry, Papa, I'll remember that."

"I hope you do. Shall I say you'll go tomorrow?"

"Yes."

So, the next day I wear my oldest tracksuit and dirtiest t-shirt and spend the day with Raffaello, a very, very nice, simple forty-five-year-old man. Married to an old friend of a friend of my parents, he is a man of few words who leads a very modest life. He works as a freelance electrician. He is his own boss and runs his own business. Work. Kids. Family. That's all. There is nothing else that bothers him, or, for that matter, that interests him.

His job is simple and skilled. I get it very quickly. I like working with him. It is exactly what I need to anaesthetise the pain and the guilt. It is a medicine for the horrible feeling my life is spinning out of my control, without me having any chance of putting it back on track.

The job is more straightforward than I expected. Raffaello looks at some electrical plans, draws lines on the white walls. He tells me how to make holes in the wall with a hammer and scalpel according to those plans. I make the holes and he follows, laying tubes for the electrical cabling. That's it. Quite clear. This is all we do for an entire day. We break for lunch for forty-five minutes and then we start again. At five we finish and go home. Before we arrive home, he pays me in cash and asks me if I want to come back tomorrow. I say for sure. He tells me he will be outside my house at half-past seven the next morning. I say I will be there, and I go back up.

After work my father waits for me in the kitchen, curious about how it went. My father was an engineer before retiring so I have entered his world for the first time. A world made of honest hard work that pays well enough to take care of one's family. That's their world. A simpler, clearer world where men work and women stay at home. Where there is no need for two salaries to have a good life. Where social progress is taken for granted, and where the kids are ALWAYS better off than their parents. Little did we know back then what the world would be like in thirty years. Back in those days Trump could have never become President of the United States, and Covid-19 and a pandemic had never been heard of since the 1920s... It felt VERY far away.

But back in those days everything felt possible.

My dad waits for me after my shower.

"Ready to give up?"

"Why?"

"It's hard work, right?"

"It is actually not that bad at all. I don't mind."

"You say that now. But you might change your mind after a week, when it gets repetitive..."

"I doubt it. It's indeed quite interesting."

"Wow. Didn't see this coming. You want to keep this job then?"

"I didn't say that, but as a summer job it's perfect. Thank you, Papi..."

My father is shocked. He calls out to my mother "Maria. Open a bottle of wine! My son is growing up. Better late than never!"

"You drink too much!" she answers back.

We all laugh.

"See? With your mother I never win."

Dinner and back to bed. As if Serena didn't exist. As if I didn't have any issues in the world. The day after it all starts again.

Every day Raffaello comes to pick me up in his spotless red van that smells so nice, buys me lunch and pays me regularly in cash every night. After a few days my mother insists on packing lunch for me, like she always does. She prepares fresh sandwiches for me and for Raffaello early in the morning before we leave. She wakes up on purpose for that at six every day. We eat them on the floor of a new house he is working on that, when finished, will look truly stunning.

The days go by. The money piles up. Raffaello warms to me and me to him. My mother's delicious sandwiches also help. A week becomes ten days. My dad is impressed, and even my skeptical mother is too. I don't give up on this raw, physical job. I don't complain. I do my job and get paid every day. As simple as that.

I don't know that this will last, but for a few days I don't think about anything. As we drive out in the mornings, I look in the opposite direction to Serena's house. I don't want to look at her garden to see if her mother's car is still parked there or if they've left to go on holiday in Southern Italy as they always do.

I also look in the opposite direction from Signora Vanessa's balcony. I don't want to look. I don't want to know if she is wondering if I am still alive or dead. I hope she is. I hope she wonders what is going on, but what we had was so life-changing that I cannot control my emotions. And having Serena come to my house the day after - I just... froze... it's something that almost made me lose my mind. Yet. It is incredible to say that I did not think about Serena once. Ever. All I had in mind was Signora Vanessa and her incredible kisses. If she did anything wrong. If she shouldn't have kissed me that way or if, perhaps, we should have just made love.

But it is pointless. Because as I pass by one evening on the way back from work, I am looking out with my arm out of the car window feeling the air and she is on the balcony in the same hot pants and the same blue t-shirt with the plunging neckline. I look up. Our eyes click. She sees me as well but manages to stay completely cool. I wave at her. She waves back. She knows and I know. I still want her, but now work conveniently makes it almost impossible for me to see her. But I can call her.

I make the sign of a phone with my hand, and she nods. A few seconds later, in the rear mirror, I can see her still on the balcony, but her husband has come out behind her. Raging in a mix of new emotions, I look back to see what he does. If he touches her, he hugs her, he kisses her, but he doesn't do anything. She goes back in, and he follows her back into the flat and the car disappears round the bend. She certainly hasn't forgotten me either. I feel it. I imagine her at the sewing machine on the table, wearing those same incredible clothes with a husband who surely doesn't desire her like I do. Surely, he doesn't. He can't.

I call her immediately, the very second I arrive home - before even saying hello to my old mother who was cooking a huge dinner for her 'worker son'. There is the working-class respect for the 'man who works' - the breadwinner: the guy who does his job as opposed to the guy who swans around reading books and taking university exams - and they fail to understand how that will ever help with finding a job. Signora Vanessa picks up the phone on the first ring, although she still sounds casual and uninterested.

I tell her straight away I want to see her. Without missing a beat, she pretends to be talking to one of her clients and tells me that sadly 'she can't accept the job' as she will be leaving for her holidays the next day. I say I have to see her tonight. She says she is already preparing dinner and it won't be possible. I insist. She tells me her husband is hungry and hangs up.

Half of me feels like taking the Vespa to go and have another look. In case there is a way of seeing her maybe downstairs as she pretends to take out the rubbish or something just as silly. In these moments I seem possessed as if I have no control of my will or my body. I am a quivering mess, only directed by lust. But the other half of me, the half that drilled holes in walls for eight hours, decides that enough is enough. So I stay home. There is just so much control I can lose. So I don't go anywhere.

I take a very cold shower... I go and kiss my parents. Lock my bedroom door and put my pillow over my head. I hardly manage not to scream. Food, as always, saves me. The smell of dinner keeps me sane. I get out of bed and have dinner as usual with my parents, smiling as if nothing had happened.

My father finishes dinner and goes down to the kitchen garden to work on his plants. I follow him, and we cut the grass together. Maybe physical work will help cleanse my mind. I read it somewhere and I feel it certainly applies to me.

The next day, Raffaello notices I seem different. Quiet. Almost silent. Admittedly not much fun to be around with, but I do my job well. The day after that I continue to do my job well and go back to being the usual regular guy who jokes and smiles and can make small talk.

But I barely say a word that whole day. Raffaello drives back to the village, past her balcony and I can see the Venetian blinds are down. No one is on the balcony. The same house full of promises and delights is now reduced to a meaningless, faceless building - with those shutters stubbornly down.

I look in the opposite direction as we drive by. Raffaello says goodbye and stops the car. Opens his wallet and pays for the last day. For this week's work in total, he has paid me the significant sum of three hundred and fifty thousand lira. Enough to buy a serious number of designer t-shirts (Ocean Pacific anyone?) or a fabulous leather jacket or, for that matter, a quarter of a new Vespa.

Are you free next week, he asks?

"I don't know. I guess it would be great to go on holiday, but I don't know what my dad would say. Can I tell you tomorrow?"

Raffaello looks surprised I don't bite his hand off - it was a very nice, generous offer. Ungrateful teenager, he must be thinking.

"Sure. Call me when you know."

"Have a nice weekend."

I go up the stairs, three at a time. I look forward to seeing my dad's face when he sees the money in my hand. The table is laid. Beautiful, and the food's warm and ready, waiting for the 'hard worker' – i.e. me. I drop the money on the table in front of my dad.

"Here goes."

"Wow, that's a lot of money."

"I told you. No messing around."

"I'm proud of you."

"Well, thank you. Now…"

"Now what? Want to quit pretending to study and become an electrician?"

Silence.

"Ahemm… No."
"Thank God. I would have been terribly disappointed."

"So… after this hard week I think I have learnt a lesson, Papa."

"Good. That was my point."

"Can I go on holiday now?"

My father smiles. And gives me a massive hug. He is such a big softie after all.

"You've earned it."

The dark cloud between us that formed a few weeks earlier with me failing my year has finally lifted. I have become the favourite son again, the lovely child my family has always been proud of. It sounds like I am about to go on holiday. Two quick phone calls to trusted Marcello, a friend from high school last year, who has a tent and an old banger of a car – so with an old tent and two sleeping bags, Liguria here we come.

I call Signora Vanessa the following morning to tell her I am about to go on holiday. Nobody answers. She is still away. Goodbye. I jump on the Vespa just to check if the shutters are down in her flat. I have to admit defeat after all.

I can't get to the sea quickly enough. Marcello comes to pick me up that evening and we drive to the seaside, the same camping ground he has been going to for the past ten years.

The sun is shining, the tent is big enough and the toilets not too bad, and it is full of girls. What more can one want?

CHAPTER 29 – What a difference a week makes

It is all very quick. The drive down to the sea with Marcello is great. We have a lot to talk about and catch up on, but then something strange happens. We realise that over the last two years we haven't gone on holiday together... and we've changed. We are different.

The rucksacks and putting up the tent are fun for Marcello, but I get impatient very quickly. I am sure he notices, but he doesn't show it. Our chats in front of the fire outside our tent under a beautifully starry sky still last all night, but they quickly become stale.

We both thought we would have so many dreams to discuss and so many plans to iron out for the following year, but the limitations of this last-minute holiday neither of us had expected become obvious. The tent isn't very comfortable. Going to the same beach every day soon becomes boring. The windsurfing classes don't go as well as we expected as we both seem really clumsy and unable to stand on the damn board for more than a few seconds at a time.

Then, the girls around the camp don't seem to like us. The music at the evening parties is too loud, and too many half-drunk dads are trying to impress their daughters and spoil the fun. The beer at the supermarket is way too expensive, and even the video games at the campsite bar don't seem right.

At night as we lie next to each other in the tent in the summer breeze under the pine trees, I can't help wondering what I am going to do next. In the middle of the night, I am not longing for Serena at all, although it occurs to me briefly that she is probably thinking the same, and perhaps she is already in someone else's arms, and I don't care.

WHHHHHHHHHAT???????

I can't believe it. After all this time and all that heartbreak. I can feel Serena is eventually ready for me, and yet all I can think of on these summer nights is a married woman thirty years older than me with whom I could never, ever have a meaningful relationship. Yet that's how it is.

WHY??????????

The first night I try to fight it. To stop thinking about her and go back to thinking about Serena. My girlfriend to be. I even try to enjoy myself: the seaside, the wind, the warm focaccia. Food. Anything to distract myself, but I can't. Signora Vanessa obsesses me more and more, and when I am able to stop thinking of her, Marcello gets in the way of my finding a way out by getting annoyed about something pointless, which brings me back to square one.

It all spells disaster, and we probably would have ended up arguing with each other if a blue bus hadn't pulled up in the half-empty car park, and then, as if in slow motion, out comes a vision from heaven: the entire bus is full of German girls arriving for their summer

188

holidays. Tall. Blonde. White skin. Different. The most beautiful girls we have ever seen in our lives, and no parents.

We have to admit the Nordic parents trust their daughters more than any Italian parent ever would.

As they climb out of the blue bus, we have never seen such short hot pants or such tight t-shirts.

We go back to our tent to make sure we look our best that evening. Best t-shirts. Best smiles. We brush our teeth and use an insane amount of cheap deodorant. The night is programmed. The same bar, but now hordes of beautiful German girls, made up and wearing outrageously sexy outfits, become the highlight of the evening. Every evening.

No need to say Marcello and his blue eyes quickly disappear with a stunning, leggy blonde bombshell called Bettina, and I somehow find myself with Inga, an impossibly tall redhead, an art lover who seems way too intellectual for the terribly unsophisticated me of twenty years ago.

We start talking about art, but let's face it, I don't really have a clue. She talks about photographers I've never heard of and visiting half the museums in London and all of the museums in Amsterdam. I have never set foot in London, but my parents have taken me to the Uffizi in Florence - does that count? Her eyes glisten. My heart starts beating faster. I talk about the little I remember and embellish what I actually remember as an incredibly boring day looking at sculptures of half-naked men in the sweltering summer heat, but I tell her about those sculptures and paintings as though I really enjoyed them - forgetting I behaved like a spoilt brat, only interested in lunch and making my father despair. Yet she has never been there, and she can't get enough details - and it doesn't matter if I am making them up. We click. She suddenly seems very interested in me and everything I have to say. A little detail: I have nothing interesting to say and cannot speak any German. She doesn't speak Italian either, but she clearly doesn't mind, and we communicate in terrible English. She is probably determined to go home and tell everybody she had a passionate Italian art lover boyfriend over the summer.

The beach is empty at night. A few faraway people are barbecuing on the sand. There is the distant sound of summer music - the kind of song you hear in Italy all during one July and August, and then not again until twenty years later; it's a classic that you dance to at someone's fiftieth birthday party, but at the time I had no idea about the future.

So, we do the whole romantic thing. She wears a very nice slightly purplish lipstick I have never seen before, and a chic pair of white trousers with a tight shirt, and heels that make her at least a foot taller than me, but she doesn't seem to mind. We walk hand in hand towards the pine forest on the edge of the beach. I bring a towel - just in case - being a good Italian middle-class boy who doesn't want the fun to get messy and be told off by mum, but she is German, and very keen to take her clothes off as soon as possible in the most messy and natural way. I clearly go along. Sand everywhere.

The sound of the sea getting closer. The sound of each other's breath as hands, limbs, lips and tongues get tangled in ways that I didn't know were possible. Rolling and kissing in the pine forest first, and then, as we grow more confident and comfortable, along the seashore and, one step further, in the sea. Even the moon shines - a long way away, but there is a blue glow, and this night is the best night of our lives - the one night we shall remember on dark winter evenings. We exchange addresses, knowing full well we shall never see each other again.

At the key moment she looks me in the eye and asks:

"Did you really enjoy your trip to the Uffizi?"

There is a naughty smile on her face, and I look down and admit "I hated the crowds and the heat."

She kisses me passionately. Right answer.

So, we have fun. Safe fun, but a lot of fun.

It is a beautiful night. I take her back, covered in sand and exhausted. The group captain, Rolf, in charge of all of fifty-two teenage girls, is still up, listening to classical music on the latest Sony Walkman.

Rolf and I look at each other. No need to say anything. We both know what just happened. He smiles. It's life.

Inga gives me a chaste kiss on the cheek and goes back in, screaming and shouting and, I am sure, exaggerating our passionate night of love.

We kept in touch, but we never see each other again. These are the moments and emotions that matter in every summer love affair.

On the way home, Marcello and I hardly say a word. We need to go back to being part-time friends who don't see each other too often.

PART 5 – September 1989 - Summer is over eventually

CHAPTER 30 – September is here

Two days after getting back, it is September. The eternal summer is finally coming to an end, and about time, but I survived!

I arrive home after the shortest and most intense holiday of my life, but two days later Inga is already a fading memory as, gradually, one after another my friends come back. Claudio arrives from the north of France with Audric. Fabrizio has another day in Sicily. All the others are back. Tanned. Happy and full of stories, made up and true. The sound of familiar motorbikes invades the warm village air again. Music to my ears. That silence I suffered alone for almost three months is finally over.

Time for answers. Time to see what I do next. Time to see if this summer has cleared my mind and cleansed my soul of the rubble I accumulated the year before. All the dramas with Signora Vanessa and Serena will come to an end - one way or another.

We still have fifteen days before school starts and I have to repeat my year, but the fun is not over yet. I don't want to think about that though. I want to jump back on the Vespa and see who is around. I think I want to see Serena, but sure as hell I have the physical need to see Signora Vanessa. Just the thought gives me a headache. I write pages and pages of my diary, but I still can't get to the bottom of it. Why can't I just forget about Signora Vanessa? Am I really that weak?

My mother wakes me up and has already made breakfast. She asks me if I want to go shopping with her. Life is back to normal. Even my father seems more benign after my slogging away as an apprentice electrician - and that paid for a good half of my holiday. My normal world is coming back.

We all knew Relo's party would be in mid-September. The party we are all waiting for to see each other after the holidays, to see who is around and who has changed - who had a nice summer and who didn't, and who stayed at home all summer, but still managed to end up in bed with a German girl - smirk.

But these were the innocent years before Facebook and selfies. There is no unkindness in the conversations we have at the Benches. People smile and hug. We are all happy to be back. The school bars reopen for business again with Mimmo and Carmelo behind the counter. The video games at the bar have changed and we have the latest version of Outrun - 'the Ferrari game with the blonde.'

We all talk, and we all smile, but deep inside of me all I want to know is when Serena is coming back, and if she is ever going to talk to me again. Even deeper inside, I also know, and I can't confess to anyone, that I drive past by Signora Vanessa's three times a day waiting for her damn Venetian blinds to go up again. How long does this woman go on holiday for? And then, just as I innocently ride my Vespa along the main road, there she is.

My heart stops even more quickly than my motor-bike. She looks amazing, of course. Yet another figure-hugging dress that I've never seen before, the same heels, and an even darker tan that makes her eyes shine even more. Oh my God. How can I cope with all of this?

We have a quick but unrushed chat... Neither of us says anything meaningful, but we can both see we have been waiting for each other. Or at least I think so - and I am seldom wrong in that department. It is obvious she knows I have been waiting for her. I just didn't expect her to be keen to see me too. Especially after what she said last time.

So, there is furious verbal sparring to see if we both still care, with the occasional glimpse of tanned skin between the slits of her skirt and the usual generous cleavage. My doubtful and slightly neurotic self is surprised she seems to have missed me too - something that I didn't see coming at all. In a couple of weeks, the balance has changed, and I can only wonder how and why. She tells me to call her again, a clear signal. No need to think. I tell her I will, and so she says we'll speak to each other soon, and I know we will.

The day after, those magic doors open to me again.

The second time I go up to her flat is completely different. I want more. I need more of that incredible kiss, but she doesn't seem to be in the mood. She seems cold, uninterested, busy. She has something else on her mind and I can feel it. We barely know each other, so she wants to talk, but I want to touch her. I am randy and impatient, but she's having none of that today.

I give up and understand that today will be about talking, and we start talking about dreams.

"My dream now is to be here, to see you like this right in front of me – that's my dream."

Pause.

I say it and mean it. Fully expecting an ecstatic, and ideally clothes-ripping passionate, panting experience, but what I get is a look of disdain.

"Are you like everyone else?" she asks.

"I thought being so young you would be different..."

She is disappointed by my shallowness and skepticism. She feels bitter about the hordes of randy Italian men who have chased her in the street and tried everything to get into bed with her.

"How can you not be a dreamer when you're so young? Can't you dream bigger? Beyond these four walls?"

She sounds critical and unnecessarily judgmental – old-fashioned almost. I step back and look at the woman in front of me again - through slightly less rose-tinted glasses. The difference in age starts creeping in, and I feel under-equipped to deal with the feelings of an obviously traditional and perhaps not as well-educated

198

woman, who is thirty years older than me. I think I'm a bit disappointed, but my mind races, looking for something to break down this wall fast.

I don't understand why she is so harsh with me. I feel warm, but also that maybe something has broken today, but then I get it - the Eureka Moment.

This is a woman who has spent half of her life being chased through the streets for the way she looks and the clothes she wears. She definitely has a reputation as a slut, and probably all the women in the village hate her. So, precisely because of this, I ask her about herself and about her work as a tailor.

Her eyes light up. Eureka.

A tiny smile appears on her lips. Without another word she goes to the fridge and makes me a water and mint syrup - deliciously refreshing and as Piemontese as it gets. She puts it in front of me, hesitates a second, and then the floodgates open.

She tells me that she was married before to a violent and controlling man who almost ruined her life. I ask how she felt when she found out she couldn't have children, and it was the biggest disappointment of her life as she always wanted to be a mother. She tells me about her friends' husbands chasing her. I know she's mine when I ask her what she would like to do one afternoon, and she says she would like to go to a field full of flowers with me and read poetry. I realise this is what we'll do next and that something special has just happened.

She tells me the intense and unusual story of her life, which is very humbling - a slow, never-ending tsunami of tragedy. I see how I underestimated and objectified this wonderful woman. Until today I had only seen an amazing body, but now I've glimpsed the soul inside, and by listening and asking questions I understand that she is teaching me a valuable lesson about life and women.

The way to her heart is to ask her about herself and about who she is and what she wants. Because no one else cares and all they do is shower her with the same cheap compliments she's already heard a million times.

Today I didn't lay a finger on her, but I know I touched her more deeply than last time in ways that I couldn't possibly understand before I ran up the stairs to her flat three at a time with my heart beating deep in my throat.

Something special happened, but I don't know what it means. I get up and she takes me to the door. Without my doing anything, she hugs me again and she kisses me on the lips again, but as her mouth opens to uncover the wonders hidden behind those lips, I feel different, and I think she feels it too. She doesn't kiss me like a little kid who somehow managed by mistake to get into her flat. She kisses me like a lover, like a person she doesn't want to leave. She kisses me like someone she will dream about tonight - lost in a flowery field, reading the poems she has wanted to hear for the last twenty years - poems that no one realised she wanted to hear.

But it doesn't last long. The kiss is over in a few beats, and in just as many beats I find myself out of the flat again. My head is spinning from the rush of blood of that second, incredible kiss. As I open the door at the bottom of the stairs, a black Mercedes Estate full of suitcases goes by with blonde girls on the backseat, one of whom happens to be Serena... but she doesn't see me.

I see her sister too.

My heart sinks. My heart sings. All at the same time. Wow. I didn't imagine this reaction at all. I literally just left Signora Vanessa, I have the taste of that kiss on my lips, and yet when I see Serena's mother's car, I have butterflies in my stomach. God. When will this roller-coaster end? Am I cheating on Signora Vanessa now? With Serena?

I put my hand up to my face, trying to wipe off invisible sweat that isn't even there.

I turn on my Vespa and look up at the balcony. Signora Vanessa is there, still in shorts and a big smile, waiting for me to wave goodbye. She blows me a kiss and goes back inside. She doesn't know what is about to happen, and I don't know either.

I ride my Vespa like a robot, knowing that unless there is really nothing left between us, Serena will recognise the engine, and so she does. Maybe I will use the horn too, like I used to. It's only three months since the holidays started, but it feels like a million years. I imagine Serena getting out of the car and hearing the noise of my Vespa, and it happens. I imagine Serena waving at me as I ride along, and it happens. I imagine riding the Vespa past her house, and I see her. She's here. For real. She sees me. She smiles. She is blonde beyond belief. She's perfectly tanned. She's wearing shorts and a t-shirt - I do think she is the most beautiful girl I have ever seen in my life.

"Ciao," she says.

"Ciao."

"Eccoci, finalmente."

"Indeed."

"Tomorrow? What are you doing?"

"Nothing. You?"

"Nothing."

"Great, so perhaps we can do some nothing together?"

She says it with a wink before her mother comes out of the house looking at me with a mildly disgusted smile, as if she had seen a zombie or a rat.

"Serena, go and unpack."

"Yes, Mum. Speak tomorrow?"

"Speak tomorrow. Shall I call you?"

"Call me. I've been waiting for you to call for the last month."

"What?"

She walks back inside. She looks at me once more before closing the door behind her. She winks and goes in.

How do girls do that?

How do they always manage to say something that makes you wonder, what if?

Is it innate? Is it something in their DNA or do they take special classes? Because this is just insane.

Tonight, will be a long night.

I go home. Have dinner. I wait for my parents to go to sleep. I go to the phone in the hall, which is not far from my parents' bedroom as we only have one phone socket. I dial the number I know by heart that ends in 9 4 2... One ring and she picks up and my heart jumps straight into my throat.

She was waiting for me to call. I sit on the floor, my back against the wall, but I feel I'm flying.

I can hear my father snoring from the bedroom, far away along the dark, silent corridor. I know this will be one of those phone calls. We start tentatively, but then a flood of words runs along the lines connecting our two houses no more than half a mile apart. After an hour she rings back. Our parents will kill us. I don't go to sleep till two. Stoned with love. Ready to pass out, but satisfied, my thirst for answers quenched. In a word... happy. Somehow. Can this be right?

CHAPTER 31 – Serena is truly back

And for the following few days we resume as if this crazy summer had never happened. I go and meet Serena every afternoon, after doing some homework I should have finished a long time ago. Just before a quiet dinner with our parents. Before dreaming of the following day again. Before quick phone calls in the night to tell each other to sleep well - before our parents yell at us to stop using the phone and curse us when they get the next phone bill.

We go back to being normal teenagers. Like we are. Like we have always been and should always have been. One boy and the girl he likes. Without any secrets. No husbands to arrive home. Without risk of causing a scandal. No need of this darkness, no need of the forbidden. We can be pure; we can continue without secrets - as we should be.

Then one day, without thinking (clearly), we just go to buy bread with the dog. Perfect idea for a walk...

My dear reader. You can see it coming, can't you? How could I not?

Now I can see it coming too, but back then, blinded by the vapours of youth and drenched in love-tinted glasses, I was taking each day as it came with the abandon of 'Carpe diem', without worrying about the implications for the future and not worrying about anyone else, including Signora Vanessa who, after that incredible, sensual kiss, saw me disappear for almost a week. I never thought what she might be thinking about me and where the hell I disappeared. I never thought about her actually missing me. Until this day and our more or less random meeting in the streets.

Me and Serena, t-shirt and shorts, holding hands in the streets. Pongo pulling us up the street, having the time of his life. Together, like any other young couple, strolling the streets of our beautiful village. We were not together officially yet, but we were less and less scared of showing we were in love. Coming down that cobbled street, smiling, chatting constantly, not a thought in our heads as we were heading to town to buy a few things for her mother – and as any other good teenagers would, talking nonstop about apartheid and what was happening in Eastern Europe.

Then I saw Signora Vanessa out of the corner of my eye, dressed in a flimsy blue dress, turning the corner and walking up to the bakery. Oh my God. What was I thinking? Serena keeps talking passionately about Nelson Mandela and the injustice of his treatment. I nod intently, telling her my opinion, but my life and the rest of that day goes into slow motion.

The embarrassment of lowering my eyes as Signora Vanessa gets closer. Seeing her in the street and seeing her eyes when she sees me with Serena. I lose the plot, but Serena takes over the conversation. My hands hold hers even tighter - unable to do anything else. The fear in my eyes as I wondered if she would make a point of saying hi to me. The horror... oh, the sheer horror as Serena says good morning to her! I couldn't care less about South Africa now; I just want this to be over.

Serena doesn't even notice and repeats that she loves talking to me because I am so well-read and opinionated - something I never thought was a particular plus before.

The blood pumping in my veins as Serena and Signora Vanessa speak to one another about a dress for Serena's mother, and they both stroke the dog - who is loving it. As if nothing had happened. As if it wasn't me in her arms a week ago in her flat, stepping, quite possibly, on her mother's dress on the floor as I kissed her in the kitchen. As if it wasn't those lips that passionately kissed me and made me feel dizzy, the same lips that last night kissed Serena outside her house - hidden in the dark. They even know each other. Signora Vanessa knows Serena and her mother. What was I thinking? But she doesn't say anything. She barely acknowledges my presence, and she just greets me with a "Ciao Alberto, say hi to your mother" - as if she knew her. Then she turns around and walks off.

Serena innocently pokes me as my eyes rest a second too long on her skirt, but we smile at each other. She tests me: "I hope you don't like old ladies, right?" Haha, I smile "Me? Are you crazy?" as I unconvincingly laugh my way out of an incredibly tight corner. Even Pongo barks at the idea. "Signora Vanessa is very nice, but the way she dresses... you know! She should tone it down a bit, don't you think?" I answer, uninterested again: "Sure... anyway... what were we saying? Nelson Mandela, right?"

Relief takes over as Signora Vanessa walks away. I feel a strange sense of rebirth as Serena squeezes my hand as if nothing happened. We just met another friend

207

of her mother - even with a particularly hot body. My heart sings as I can see that Serena didn't notice anything and continues, but this is not over yet as I feel my head turning and looking at Signora Vanessa walking away.

In incredible slow motion the sense of sheer dread returns as Signora Vanessa must feel my eyes on her as she walks away towards the shops and turns towards me, and before Serena can turn, right in the middle of the village roads, probably surrounded by dozens of bored eyes, hungry for any saucy gossip, she blows me a little kiss. The kiss glides in the air slowly and reaches me nevertheless with the power of the punch of a heavyweight boxer.

I close my eyes as I feel the hit and smile at Serena nonchalantly, listening to her talk about her friend's struggle to finish her homework, but I don't hear a word that she is saying. My mind is racing.

I think about what it means to this young heart and this young girl who once again is giving me an opportunity to love her in a clean and pure manner. Do I want this pure love, or do I want to sink in the darkness of forbidden love? Why can't I just focus on the innocent talk about homework. What is it that I am looking for? Why can't I just say no to this dark and dangerous excitement?

Serena tells me off for looking at this old lady who is older than her mother and always showing off, but how she is a really good tailor, but "those dresses she wears are brilliant publicity but no other woman in the village has a body like hers..." so the same dresses look horrible on all the other women with bigger thighs, smaller breasts, larger waists and less toned backs. We both laugh.

I answer distractedly - uninterested. As if Serena's comments don't concern me, and she quickly goes back to her friend and her homework. I even give my opinion. As if her comments about that body I spent the summer dreaming of, don't concern me, as I'm not already thinking about her body - as if I don't feel like going to reclaim the kiss she blew me while I was holding Serena's hand.

But Signora Vanessa must have seen in my eyes as she blew that kiss that I was going to ring her bell immediately after dropping Serena at home - feeling more excited but also more drenched in sin than ever. Signora Vanessa must have known, and because she knew I was coming, she ignores my ringing at her bell and leaves me outside. Gagging for more. Punishing me for my temerity of being myself, just a teenage boy who is trying to explore the world in the arms of a girl his own age - as opposed to a full-blown woman thirty years his senior with all the knowledge and the secret skills to drive his naive young mind crazy.

I know I have to try harder. I have to think. I have to make more of an effort... to be allowed back in the flat of a married woman while I am courting a seventeen-year-old girl whom I have desired for years - and to hide it all.

That evening I miss the phone call with Serena, shaking from desire for Signora Vanessa. Lost in plans about how to intercept her the following day. My mind and soul are fighting one another, making me more confused than ever.

The phone rings late at night. I know it is Serena, but my father is still up, and he answers before I can do anything. She hangs up. My father curses people who call at midnight and goes to bed. I wait for the phone to ring again, but it doesn't.

So, I fall asleep - right by the phone.

She does ring again a few moments later and I answer in a millisecond. Then I wait to see if my father is going to wake up again and curse people who call late at night.

I imitate my father's voice "Are you one of those people who call late at night?"

We both laugh and spend the next two hours on the phone. I clearly remember that when the next telephone bill came my father was so angry that I had to go and get a part-time job with Raffaello for a few weekends. I had to pay 75% of that bill, and it taught me a couple of lessons. First that it only took two days' work to pay what appeared to be an enormous phone bill. Second not to leave bad feelings behind. Whatever the cost. Always say one word more rather than one word less. This has served me really well in life.

CHAPTER 32 – Signora Vanessa is back too

The next day I really become a cheat. Much to my disgust and to my horror when I think back. This is a chapter I am definitely not proud of.

After yet another sleepless night spent writing my diary and forcing myself to just focus on the light that Serena is bringing into my life, for whatever reason I jump on the Vespa and somehow the motorbike takes on a life of its own and stops by Signora Vanessa's home.

I stand in front of the house, staring at the doorbell for quite a while, fully knowing I shouldn't be there. I have every reason not to be there, but there am. I ring, but she won't open the door. Literally and metaphorically. I telephone her. She answers and tells me she is busy. Then she hangs up. All this anticipation is over in a few seconds.

It drives me crazy, and somehow it makes me more determined than ever.

Serena comes round to my house on her bicycle. An ideal opportunity to forget it all. I meet her. I speak to her, but my mind and most of my body are dreaming of the older woman who could be my mother. My rational mind tells me this is all wrong and I should stop this madness straight away, but I can't. We pedal out to the country in the sunshine, the wind in our faces, looking for a quiet field full of flowers where we can hide and kiss romantically, away from gossipy eyes, parents and friends who are way too keen on finding ways to separate us.

And it is in the middle of the field that I again have an almost physical reaction of rejection. Much as I enjoy kissing this innocent and beautiful girl in these perfect surroundings, my body cringes as I know how badly I want the other woman, and so I find an excuse to go back home. I don't feel good about it. I really don't.

It is my relationship with Serena that haunts me the most. Here she is. Blonde. Young. Tanned. More beautiful than ever and, after so many years, ready to be with me. She hasn't told me clearly yet, but I feel it. In the way she looks at me when she sees me. In the way she tries to ring me and meet me on every occasion, and somehow the more I hide, the more she comes chasing after me, looking for reasons to meet up: watching a film, going for a walk, even, astonishingly, watching football together. Serena has never watched football before in her life. This must be real love.

Then the bomb. One afternoon Serena and her friends mention they will go to the next Vasco Rossi concert in two weeks. We are watching a film in her living room, and Serena asks if I want to go. I have never been to a Vasco concert, but this sounds like one I cannot miss. It sounds like the most romantic day ever. Serena and me, surrounded by twenty thousand people, singing the songs we've always sung together. What more could I want?

But then, I want to be in that flat again.

My Vespa goes by, and there is Signora Vanessa on her balcony, and she sees me. I am sure by now she recognises my engine. Fearlessly and without any shame I turn around and park in front of her building. She smiles and goes back into her flat, waiting, I am sure, for me to ring her bell.

I ring, and for the first time she doesn't even ask who it is. She just opens the door.

Two flights of stairs and I'm in.

I don't even let her open her mouth. As soon as I've closed the door behind me, I hug her, I hold her, I kiss her. She lets me, and she kisses me back with passion, like a lover - not like a little kid anymore. I have never been kissed this way and she knows it. It is my first kiss with a real woman, and I'm fully aware that I am just one very thin layer of cotton away from having her naked, alone, in her flat with an abundance of sofas and beds on which to abandon ourselves - should the opportunity arise. We melt into each other. Every other thought just disappears - lost in this moment that maybe will last forever even though, in reality, it cannot have lasted more than five minutes.

But then again, she challenges me.

"And then?"

"And then what?"

I repeat, barely able to breathe after what was the most sensual experience of my life so far.

"Now that you've kissed me... so what happens next?"

I stutter "I actually have no idea... I can barely breathe..."

"You know what I would like now?"

"Anything you want, and I'll get it for you."

"Very well. I would like you to take me to a field full of flowers and I want you to kiss me there."

"I don't understand."

This is not what I was expecting. I was expecting a woman full of passion and burning carnal desires who would revel in my youth exuberance, but no. Again. This is not how women function.

She tells me how men feel about her. How they all want to take her to bed. How all the women in the village hate her because they think she's after their husbands.

I argue that perhaps the way she dresses may have something to do with it - not that I'm complaining- but she's in yet another pair of barely-there shorts and a top with a neckline as wide as a football pitch. Again - not that I'm complaining.

She smiles. Clearly, she has heard all this before. She says she was given this body and she likes to dress as she pleases. She tells me that she is on her second marriage - that her first husband was very controlling, very jealous and also very violent.

I look at her with different eyes.

This is not what I was expecting.

I thought she was going to give me passion, but she wants poetry. I thought she was going to rip my clothes off, but she is wearing more than ever. I thought we were going to have a day of wild sex, yet we are talking very politely at her kitchen table with biscuits and a cup of tea. If her husband were to walk in now, he probably wouldn't feel suspicious at all. Just a young boy who came to pick up a dress for his mother.

But this is not what she is expecting either.

As I grow older, I understand the power of my actions and the impact they have on people, but back then I was totally oblivious. I saw myself as a little boy in the hands of a far more experienced woman, who surely knew what to do and who was totally unaffected by the waves of emotion breaking over me.

As always, the minute I get there she wants me to leave. It was her defense mechanism. To try and push away something that was probably too much for her to deal with. Something exciting yet dangerous that could have destroyed so much more of her life than mine. It must have been weird for her to cook dinner for her husband as if nothing had happened, minutes after a hormonal eighteen-year-old just left her flat.

"Alberto, you must leave."

I hear the words with dread, and they come every time. I can't understand why.

"But I just got here."

"I know. But you must go."

"Why?"

"Because I say so."

"Don't give me the usual. You must leave if you want to come back..."

She smiles.

"You know, you are a very cheeky mister!"

"Am I?"

She gets close.

"You know when men see me in the street, they sound the horn as they see me from behind as they expect me to be a young girl. When they see me as I am, a mature woman, most of them drive off. Some of them even insult me and shout" Vecia - old lady – "why the hell do you dress like that? Who do you think you are?" as if they should decide how I dress. As if I hadn't spent all my life designing these dresses and tailoring them to myself and my body. I know my body. I know what it does to men. But just because they feel like that, it doesn't mean I feel that way.

I look down. I've heard it all myself. I've heard all the casual comments at the bakery. Which normally start the minute she leaves the shop.

She knows it too. I know that, but it hurts her nevertheless.

"But you know what I really want from a man?"

I look down again. I honestly have no idea what a woman like this needs from a man. I barely know at eighteen what it means to be a man.

"I want a man who reads me a poem - written just for me. I am forty-six years old, and no one has ever done that for me."

The little boy that I was smiled. The man I am today smiles even more about how little we men understand women and what they need.

It was a revelation to me. The tougher the woman, the more sexually aggressive on the outside, normally the softer and more vulnerable her heart. The clothes, the sex appeal, even the sex is often just a shield designed to protect a soft heart from the harm our tough world can inflict. An innocent girl was hidden behind that very sensual and sexual exterior. A simple, innocent girl who had been hurt by the twists and turns of fate.

That was how she was. Nothing more and nothing less, but I was too young to appreciate what any of this meant.

"What is it that you want, Alberto? What is your dream in life? The real one. Don't tell me something cheap…"

"I want to go to London… to film school."

There. I'd said it.

"But I don't know if we can afford it. It's incredibly expensive, and I don't know if I am actually talented enough to go to film school…"

She gets close to me. I see her eyes glint. She locks them on mine and doesn't let go. My palms are sweating again - the silence is electric - every cell of my body is ready for whatever is about to happen… Or is it?

"You have the talent to do anything, Alberto. Be confident. Have faith. I trust you. You can do it. Believe in yourself… and, most importantly, believe in the power of your dreams."

"Thank you. Tonight, I needed this."

"You know, Alberto. Tonight, I got a tip about a brand of American trainers called LA Gear. Ever heard of them?"

I shake my head.

"I feel this is the investment that will allow me to live my dream. To go to Australia at last. I have been working on this for almost ten years. Learning about the stock market, buying and selling shares while the whole village sees me as nothing but a sex object and a husband-stealer. Even you see me that way. You know the only man who sees me differently? For what I really am? My husband... he understands everything... a shame he is so cold, but no one is perfect, you know. I have to go my own way. Regardless of what anyone else thinks. I believe you should do the same. Remember these words: believe in the power of your dreams."

And with one swift move, as if throwing a horny teenager out of her flat was second nature to her, she bundles me out and there I am going down those marble steps again.

The air is cool outside the door. My motorbike is still there.

But against the backdrop of a dark sky with thick clouds, I see a little hand-written note on the seat and shiver.

Who could have left a hand-written note on my seat?

I look at it closely. It's in a girl's handwriting - round letters and balls dotting the 'I'. I don't recognise it though.

I don't think I want to read it there. So I put my helmet on and ride off, my heart beating faster than ever, not knowing what to expect. I go to the Benches. A few

219

friends drive by on their motorbikes. I sit on a bench by myself away from everybody and I open the note which is addressed to me.

"What the f*** are you doing? Do you really think that no one has noticed? Do you really want to ruin your life?"

I start to sweat.

"You have a wonderful, innocent girl waiting for you in her bedroom. She dreams of you. You are the first man in her life. The only one, and you chase an old woman that could be your mother? What the f*** is wrong with you? If you don't pull yourself together a note like this will go to Serena - and your mother. Then you will see what will happen."

"Wake up. You deserve better!"

Signed: "a friend who believes in you."

I jump back on my motorbike almost another person. I am doing something wrong, and I know that, but this 'friend' has slapped me in the face and given me a wakeup call.

People are watching. People know. Should I worry?

CHAPTER 33 - The friends you find and those you choose

That night I come home to dinner with my parents. As always. I arrive on time. I'm usually late. My father is quite impressed. Very unusual of me to turn up on time. My mother serves the food. Beans minestra and chicken fillet with vegetables. One of my favourites, yet I don't feel much like eating. I have to force myself. The leftovers will do for Pongo, who is used to eating everything we give him.

My mother asks me if everything is ok and I grunt a distracted yeah, but I wonder what she would say if only she knew. She talks about school again. She and my dad must have been talking about that. My final year of high school. We need to think about university soon. I know, I say, distracted. Something else much bigger is in my head, but I can't talk about that with either of them.

These are the moments that define your life. This is probably one of the first. I have always been a nice boy who doesn't want to hurt anybody, especially my parents. So, sometimes the best way of keeping the status quo is to tell a white lie. Stay out of trouble.

But you can't lie forever. Especially to the ones you love. Because when they look you in the eye, if you see disappointment, it is the worst feeling possible.

So that night I decide. I have to stay away from Signora Vanessa. Come what may. Now I know.

The friend who believes in me has already made a big difference, but how long will my willpower last? And more importantly, how will I fill my days and nights? And, even worse, will she even notice?

I need to talk to someone about this. I really do.

Fabrizio and me at the Sottosopra, our reliable and wonderful local gastro-pub - Italian-style of course. Where you order from a limited selection of drinks (a half-pint of a little-known Swiss beer), but you have an amazing choice of food such as raw Fassone beef with fresh asparagus and truffles... Say no more.

I have trouble approaching such a delicate subject. Fabrizio thinks for a bit, and we look at each other. He smiles as he ties the laces of his Air Jordan shoes and just says "Certain things happen because they have to happen."

The next evening: me, Claudio and Fabrizio. Same pub. Same drinks. Different food. Just burgers and fries. Beer. Me and Claudio together. I still don't know how to introduce the subject. I decide that being direct is the best way. He smiles as his brand-new mobile phone, the size of a brick, beeps, and everybody looks at him. He appears to be a very important man rather than a spotty, spoilt teenager, and his reaction is very different. He answers like the older brother he is. Other people would say he sounds like a man talking to a boy - me.

"You're a dickhead. What do you see in her? She could be your mother. Seriously, do you have motherly issues?"

"What are you talking about?"

Back to Fabrizio... "Thanks, but what do you mean?"

"That the little piece of paper from 'the friend' must be fate. You are doing something wrong that could hurt more people than you realise - maybe including yourself. So, fate is telling you that you should stop. What do you think?"

"I think I want her so much that I don't think I can stop."

"Well... the fates are telling you something. Maybe if you are doing this it is because there was a need, something in you that needed this. There is no right or wrong, just follow your instincts and you'll find the way."

Pause.

"Tell me again. I'm lost..."

Back to Claudio...

"I think you are totally crazy. Do you want to ruin your life? Why are you risking everything over something so stupid? Sometimes I don't know what is in your head. For God's sake, c'mon! Show some balls..."

"Are you always so angry?"

"You make me angry when you say these stupid things…"

Back to Fabrizio…

"I think if this is what you really, really want, maybe you should go for it, but at the same time be fully aware of what you are doing. And choose either one or the other… but listen to destiny… it is trying to talk to you right now…"

"Again?"

"Well, how do you feel about it, morally?"

"Morally?"

"Quite important to think about that. Don't you think?"

Back to Claudio…

"Show some balls and never see her again! You are about to go out with Serena. Remember? This is what you have always wanted and have been busting my balls over for the last three years. Now you have her, and you're chasing someone who could be your mother…"

Back to Fabrizio…

"Are you clear about what the fates are telling you to do?"

Back to Claudio…

"Are you clear about what your brain is telling you to do?"

They both look at me.

I smile. Clear. As mud.

"Thanks, guys!"

Two evenings later I leave the same pub with some other friends and, just outside the swinging wooden doors, I bump into Marcello. I haven't seen him since our seaside adventure with the German girls. He is with a crowd I don't know. We say ciao, and hug like the good old friends we are, even if the holiday didn't quite work out the way we planned.

Both our sets of friends go on ahead and we're alone for a second. I feel he is holding our hug for a second too long, as if we have a big secret to tell each other. Something is up, but I don't know what he wants to say.

Marcello looks around and lowers his voice conspiratorially.

"Alberto?"

"Yes?"

"Tell me something I've been dying to ask you..."

"I'm all ears..."

He looks around again as if this is a big, big secret...

"Don't ask me how I know, but I hear that you are hanging around with the…" he lowers his voice even more, if that's possible. I can barely hear him…

"The sexy tailor… the older lady…"

My jaw hits the ground! I am speechless. I thought I was being so careful, and then I get an anonymous letter, and a friend stops me at the pub to talk about it. W T F!

"Do people know?"

"No, no. Don't worry. Your dirty little secret is safe. You old dog…"

"So how do you know?"

"I've seen your motorbike outside her block of flats a few times and, to be honest, my mother goes there to get her trousers altered. Also, I saw you talking to her in the village - outside the bakery."

"And?"

"You were eating her alive… Man, you were…"

Gosh! I swallow. Not sure I can take another judgment tonight…

"I wanted to say well done!"

What?

"You're a real man! I wish I had the balls to do what you do."

I look at him. Confused.

"I wish I had the balls to go and see a real woman like that in her flat. Bang her every day before her husband comes home..."

My jaw drops again. Is that what they think we are doing in her flat? I am so shocked - and probably more than a bit flattered - that I can't tell him the truth. I don't want to spoil his image of macho me seducing a desirable, sexy, older woman.

He whispers "Alberto..."

"Yes?"

"Tell me, what is she like in bed? Wild?"

"Marcello..."

I can see Marcello salivating over the gossip I am about to relay, and I can't help saying

"She does things..."

"Yes?"

He is panting by now with excitement...

"That I cannot even repeat..."

His eyes widen so much that they almost explode. He shakes his head, imagining God knows what.

"Your secret is safe with me, brother."

We stand back and look at each other. We hug again. The holiday is a long-lost memory, but tonight there is a new level of respect, and we go back to our respective friends.

CHAPTER 34 – The end of summer party at "the base"

The day of Relo's birthday party eventually arrives. Everybody is so happy to go. All the girls are back. We wonder who is going out with whom now. We all look around. The school bar becomes a busy teenage playground again. The Benches are full of young people keen on talking, mixing, exchanging their experiences of a long summer. There is a secret place in the middle of the forest we call 'the base', and it's there we decided to have a barbecue that night.

Serena's pain-in-the-backside mother won't let her come, so I am on my own. All the other girls are there. Everybody is there. Cristina is super-hot, wearing purple lipstick that I still remember twenty years later, but she is with someone else, and everything is going almost perfectly. Marcello, whose dad is a butcher, has brought twenty kilos of delicious sausages, chops and all sorts of other wonderful meaty things. Vegetarianism was very rare back then. We park the motorbikes in one corner and someone starts building the fire. A few of the girls help Claudio with the cooking. Two guys open the cases on their motorbike, and they are full of beer. Other people bring some more food. Somebody has brought a radio. Somebody else starts singing. The forest resonates with rock music and happy young people. We dance. We drink. We say silly things. We smoke cigarettes and joints. Everybody is dressed up in their best clothes and the party is cool.

I look around. Serena is still nowhere to be seen, but I realise with pleasure that there are a lot of other girls I've never noticed before who seem quite keen on me.

One of them is very keen. Her name is Laura, dark hair, tall and skinny - an ex-ballerina. She is wearing those skintight black leggings that are very fashionable this summer, and she has nice long legs. She still dances and she is intelligent and witty - very interesting indeed. Marcello goes by and winks at me.

"C'mon, you lion, leave some girls for us..." he says and walks away.

Laura looks at me, not sure what Marcello meant, and nor am I.

As our party is wrapped in darkness, the group breaks into couples. Some start kissing. I'm one of the few whose girl hasn't turned up.

After the summer I've just had, how can I go back to being who I was before? To discussing school marks innocently, and going to university, to deciding what to do in the future? I feel I have so much more to do and feel. I have experienced so much more. I try to speak to Laura who, in the black of the forest, is pure, intelligent and witty, if a bit dull. We talk and talk. It would be very easy to kiss her but, somehow, I don't feel like it.

I enjoy the electricity of this obvious attraction, but because I am not interested, I am more than capable of playing supercool. I wish I could keep this cool with

Serena, but I am gradually getting used to thinking one clear, rational thing and ending up doing the opposite.

So that night after the party, when it's past midnight and I'm slightly drunk, I write a poem. I must say that as I pour my heart out, I have no idea who I am writing for. I realise an old woman asked me for a poem a few days ago, but this poem takes on a life of its own as I write. Page after page, attempt after attempt. The words flow by themselves. I don't even know what has inspired this poem. After a few hundred tries I come up with this:

It is quite scary to write these lines to you
What do I call you? My love? My fancy?
My dear?
My heart?
And yet my feelings for you are so clear.
From that day on the bicycle across the village,
Wearing that marvellous blue dress,
Every moment is carved indelibly in my heart.
With you, my heart pounds.
My head spins.
My body follows.
Every time I'm next to you I start a journey,
To another world, a different world.
A world without limits.
A world of delight, pleasure, beauty.
I don't know if it makes any sense,
I don't know if we have any future,
And I don't care.
All I have is here and now,
In the moment.
Just to see you for a few more fleeting seconds

And evoking those incredible feelings again...
That in my short life of eighteen years,
No one has been able to inspire.
I don't want this to change,
I don't want this to end.
I just long to be lucky enough to have another chance.
Another day,
Another moment with no future,
But to feel what I'm feeling.
Once more.
Once again.
Just once.
It's all that matters now and in eternity.

I spent the whole night writing it. Word by word. Rewriting it a million times. Starting and restarting again until the sun came up. Why did I write it? I have no idea. I'd tried so many times before to write something, but somehow, I always stopped after a few lines. It just didn't make sense, but this one... just cascaded, more and more. There were another two pages, but I decided to cut it, otherwise it was going to be a novel rather than a poem.

Now, holding the handwritten poem, I feel a bit silly. What if she laughs at me? The usual fear of the misunderstood writer. But today I don't hesitate, just like a samurai. No regrets.

I put it in her mailbox in the morning, before my parents even wake up.

I imagine every moment. The moment she picks up the envelope - the surprise. She reads it. The delight. The amazement. This is something she really wanted. She is going to be really, really touched. I wrote it for her.

The phone rings.

I ignore it. I'm too busy daydreaming.

Ring!

"Alberto?" my mother says, "why don't you answer? Who do you think it's for?"

Ring!

"I'm busy, Mother. Please can you answer it?"

She stops cooking - is she always cooking, day and night?

And she goes to answer the phone. Then she opens the door and just gives me that look, telling me she was right, and I was wrong. As always...

I pick up the phone and fake annoyed.

"Hello?"

"Hello, my dear poet..."

Oh my God... Signora Vanessa's voice sounds different this morning - my heart skips a beat, and I don't seem to be able to say a word. A croak comes out of my mouth.

"Mmmfffffhhh?"

That warm voice I know so well doesn't give up. Maybe the poem has something to do with it?

"Still alive?"

A long silence.

"Barely."

"I'm glad. It took me some time to find you and courage to call with a remotely plausible excuse..."

"Plausible excuse... I see... And?"

"And?"

We say it at the same time... We stop. We laugh. We people from Torino are so polite.

"Ladies first," she continues.

"Of course," I say.

"And... the reason why I called you..."

"Exactly what I was wondering..."

"Is that I wanted to say thank you, of course... and..."

"And?"

"I want to see you again."

A very long silence.

"So, what you are saying is that I now, after a poem, can come to your house?"

"Maybe..."

"I will ring the bell... and you will just open...?"

"If I am free..."

"Of course, and unless you've changed your mind again..."

Pause.

"Alberto..."

Way too eager... "Yes?"

"Don't spoil it."

Silence.

"Ok."

"Why don't you come over tomorrow afternoon? Maybe we can watch a film together?"

I can't believe she said that. How do I end this conversation?

"I'll wait for you to call then," she says.

"Speak tomorrow."

"Sure. Sleep well…"

Another pause.

"If I can…"

"I am sure you'll manage."

Click.

The following morning, we are back at school, but the afternoon can't come fast enough.

CHAPTER 35 – Back to school

The school bus that morning felt like the hurricane in the United States. The walk to the square with the fountain. The crowd of the same people with their usual colourful Invicta rucksacks decorated with mottos handwritten in permanent marker. The motorbikes, the cars, the bicycles. The jokes, the laughter, the banter, the flirting, the chatter. Everybody is happy to go back to school in September, and almost happy to see the same teachers - or at least some of them. Even they seem relaxed and happier after a couple of months without us. I'm changing class – it's the year after I failed, but it feels like a lifetime ago. The headteacher, Professoressa Pezzani is waiting at the entrance, surveying the swarm of students, and she smiles at me. I'm sure she will keep an eye on what I do this year – it's make or break.

I know several of my new classmates anyway, and there's the same familiar feeling of teachers sizing me up. They must have heard all about the crazy guy who failed everything in the last months, but I don't seem to bite and I'm not disrespectful, so they leave me alone. Or maybe it's just the first day.

Claudio is one year ahead so he's going to university. We'll catch up in the holidays. Fabrizio is one year behind, so he has one more year of suffering in the mountains before going to university in Torino - and eventual freedom.

The classes go swiftly, one after another. The usual routine. The breaks. The books. Plans for the football team. Training resumes. Sunglasses come out on the way home. The boys and girls check each other out on the way out of school.

Serena on the bus back home.
One quick look.
A smile.

The kids come and go. We meet in the breaks; our shoulders brush, but we mostly ignore each other. I am meant to go to her house this afternoon, so no need to rush anything.

In fact, no, I will not sit next to you on the way back today. She smiles. She knows this game. We both know the game we're playing today. We both know that this year something feels different somehow. Yet she doesn't know what is inside me.

Maybe it's the tan or the confidence. Maybe it is what I felt at Relo's party with Laura. To pretend I am not interested is a way of learning how to play it cool and apparently uninterested. Does it work? Something is different. Maybe Inga has done something to my confidence and Serena can sense it. Maybe Signora Vanessa has. A shame it has to be secret and slightly sordid. I wish it were different. I wish I were strong enough to tell Signora Vanessa to get lost and to lose myself in the arms of this beautiful girl who, after three years and an Interrail pass across Europe, brought me back a piece of the Berlin Wall that has ended up as one of my father's treasured possessions in a handmade case.

On the bus I sit with Fabrizio. We are in different classes, so we have a lot to catch up on. Serena sits with her friend Francesca, so even if I wanted to, I could not sit next to her. Fabrizio and I talk about what we will do at the weekend: Another party somewhere nearby - apparently a villa with a swimming pool. Everybody will be there. I can't wait. This is our life after all.

Fabrizio gets off at the bus stop at the beginning of the village and I sit alone for the rest of the trip. I put my headphones on and listen to Madonna on my Walkman. The tape was a birthday present. The dance music goes to my head as I dream of this afternoon. I must make the phone call. I think of that as Serena smiles at me. She keeps an eye on me and sticks her tongue out, but, really, she has no idea what I am thinking. Maybe I feel this is another way to play it cool and attract her attention.

The bus arrives at the final stop, and only then she speaks to me: "Alby?"

"Yes?"

"Did you buy a ticket for the concert? Because I think they are selling out..."

"I'll go this afternoon..."

"Don't put it off..."

"I won't. I wouldn't miss it for the world."

"You'd better not!"

"See you later?"

"See you later."

And in a magical moment, without any warning or notice, she just briefly, quickly, kisses me on the lips and runs away. I have no time to say anything. No reaction. But the sparks were there. I touch my lips with my finger, almost struggling to believe it happened.

We walk towards our homes. My gate opens before I even ring the bell, and my mother is waiting for me - the first lunch after the summer holidays. A massive, smoking plate of pasta is ready with Bolognese sauce and a mountain of Parmesan.

I walk up the stairs and drop my rucksack in the doorway, and what happens next is indelibly etched in my memory. I kiss my mother and go to the bathroom to wash my hands, but I don't see my dad lying on the sofa.

"Mamma, where is Papa?"

He has never not been there for lunch with me since he retired five years ago.

"He's still asleep. I tried to wake him up, but he doesn't answer."

"Papa sleeping at half-past two in the afternoon? When I get home?"

These offhand words from a woman who is more worried about her meal staying warm than anything else freak me out. My father is lying on the dining room sofa in front of the TV and looks as though he is asleep, but he doesn't answer me. I slap his face gently, but he doesn't react. This is strange.

I freak out.

"Papa?"

No answer.

"Papa!"

Time stops. I realise this is one of those moments when life changes. I look at my father's face. He looks white and in pain. Not like he's sleeping. This is exactly what happened when he ended up in hospital and had a triple bypass. Is this another heart attack?

"Papa! Wake up!"

A drop of cold sweat rolls down my spine as I fear the worst, but then I feel a strange calm inside. As if I'm no longer the ridiculous student only worried about chasing a girl. I'm a cool, cold-blooded adult. And in control.

"We need to call an ambulance. I think he's had another heart attack."

Only then did my mother stop cooking to take a closer look at the husband she had almost lost once before.

She reacts in slow motion, only just realising what has happened and why my dad is not responding. She can't take it in, but this one telephone call may save my father's life.

We hear the ambulance siren as it gets closer. This is a quiet residential road, so all the neighbours are watching. The paramedics arrive quickly, and the nurse realises this is very serious. Everything seems to be going on in the background: my uncle comes up to ask what has happened; the neighbour opposite makes the sign of the cross - maybe she'll pray for him. My mother packs a bag with necessities in less than five minutes. I climb into the back of the ambulance, and we zip off to hospital in a glare of flashing lights and blazing sirens. The neighbours look through their windows as the ambulance drives off. I concentrate on my father with an oxygen tube in his mouth. Nothing else counts. The paramedic checks for signs of life. It's all a blur, but I hear the words 'brain damage'. My father is taken straight to A&E, and I go too. 'Intensive care', 'defibrillation' - I have to wait outside.

I know my father is hovering between life and death as I sit there, suddenly the man of the family. It was probably then, alone at the hospital, not knowing if I was going to be an orphan, that I grew up. Learning the importance of the moment and of the people. Learning that everything else can stop, but not caring for the people whom you love and who love you. Everything else can wait. Also, the importance and the power of trusting other people. You have to trust the doctors and just... wait.

Then I understand the value of keeping your mind busy, so you don't go crazy. I go to the café for a sandwich, a bottle of water and the newspaper. The more I worry about my father, the more I focus on the football news - as if an article about the struggles of Torino FC could alleviate the fear of my father dying. Like a few months before, I face my fears alone: at eighteen I am way too young to be an orphan, but it could happen today, and I would not have a father any more. I think about when I last spoke to him. I think about the fact that the night before we didn't even watch TV together because I was too obsessed with Serena and Signora Vanessa. I think about the last words I said to him. Did I ever tell him how much I love him and that I am not ready for life without him? But tonight is not his last night after all. The doctor comes out and calls my name:

"Soriani?"

I stand up and walk towards him. He looks very serious.

"That's me. I'm his son."

I look into his eyes, trying to guess what he is about to tell me - but maybe not really ready to hear the worst...

"Well, your father is..."

Breathe. Breathe. Breathe.

"...much better."

Oh my God, thank you. Thank you. Thank you!

"He needs to spend a night in hospital, but he is recovering. It was just a minor stroke, and there is no damage. He was very lucky - another hour and he might have died. You called the ambulance?"

"Yes, I did."

"Well, bravo. You saved his life."

"May I see him?"

"Not yet, but we'll let him out of intensive care in a few hours. You can see him then, but don't worry. He's out of danger."

I sit down again. Gripping my newspaper, almost passing out. I spend that night in the hospital with him. Waiting for him to be allowed out. I call my mother on a pay phone. She has already told my uncles and all our relatives, and a couple of my dad's best friends are on their way. This is also typical of my dad. His network. He is never alone. Whenever he needs something, there will always automatically be someone who moves in to help. This is the man he is. Always willing and ready to help without anyone asking. So, his beautiful karma works for him too. I learnt this from him and have tried to replicate it. Always help. Pick up the phone. Check if someone is ok. Because this is what makes a difference to someone's life. We are all in this together, and it is always better to make one phone call too many than regret the one you didn't make.

My uncles Leonino and Nevio arrive and try to persuade me to go back home and sleep. It feels so different to just a few weeks ago when they were arguing about communism, but I want to stay there at the hospital with him. I want to be there when he wakes up. They let me sleep for a couple of hours on the sofa in the waiting room, and then a few hours and a few coffees later I'm back there. Waiting, but at least I'm not alone now.

The door of the intensive care unit opens, and there he is, joking with a blonde nurse. We stand up even before they call our names. I can see him looking for me. I go and hold his hand...

"Ciao, Alberto."

"Papa..."

My uncles - his brothers - gather around me.

"We're all here."

"What is this? A reunion? Don't you have anything better to do?"

"Did you think we'd let you come here alone? You know the coffee here is so good that we had to come too," jokes my Uncle Nevio, the family comedian.

He laughs.

The nurses take him to a normal room. He is out of danger.

"He needs to rest. Follow me, please. He just needs to sleep, and then in the morning the doctor will visit him."

We all follow him.

"No, no. Sorry. Only one person at a time is allowed in."

My uncles hold my dad's hand and kiss him on the cheek.

"Ciao, Remo. See you back home in a few days."

"Alberto, we will come again tomorrow morning."

"Go, Uncle. Not to worry. I'm here. I'll go and get my mother tomorrow too."

"Great. I'll be here at eight in the morning so you can go get some rest.

"Thank you. See you tomorrow."

They leave. The strength of a big traditional family when there are health issues. The warmth. This is what I remember.

We go into his room, and I can see my dad is not himself. Maybe the stroke has affected him, but nothing seems quite what it was. He is very agitated, but the nurse gives him some medicine which calms him down a bit.

It makes me wary. There are another two men, more or less his age, in the room. We say good evening, but keep to ourselves. Then, out of the blue, my dad erupts:

"Alberto!"

"Papa," I whisper, "I'm here. Is everything ok?"

It is almost eleven after all.

"Alberto…"

He stares at the empty wall in front of his bed.

"Papa…"

"What did you do with the TV set?"

I look at the wall. There is no TV there. At first, I'm confused, but then I realise that maybe it's the medicine, and the TV set is in his mind.

"Papa, there is no TV…"

But he won't listen and raises his voice.

"Look what you've done. I told you to set the TV up properly. You're always the same!"

I can see the other two men in their beds realise what's happening. There is no point saying anything to someone who is not himself, but he's not finished yet.

"You're always the same. Can't you see? The TV's all wonky. See what happens when you do things in a rush? You don't pay attention to detail. You need to do things properly, Alberto."

Only then do I see the funny side of the story: my dad, barely out of a coma after a stroke that could have killed him, still has the energy to tell me off about a TV set that only exists in his imagination yet feels real to him. This TV almost becomes a metaphor for my life: my father is telling me what to do, how to be a man, how to become a responsible man. Alone in the hospital room. He's getting better, but what if something happens to him? Is this it? Should I call a nurse?

"You have to stop being wishy-washy, Alberto. Do things properly from beginning to end. That is what your mother and I have been trying to teach you."

I look down and smile, and I tell him what he already knows.

"I'm sorry, Papa. I will fix it in the morning, ok? I'm so sorry I let you down, but I promise I'll take care of everything in the morning. When you wake up the TV will be fixed, but now sleep, ok? It's late."

"Ok, ok. But promise me you will. You know we need TV, ok? When you're gone, it is all me and your mother have left…"

"Of course, I will, Papa. Sleep now though."

"Ok, ok. Buonanotte. Alberto?"

"Yes?"

"Have Juventus won?"

"Papa, I don't know..."

"Whom did they play?"

I have no idea how he can think about football now,
but he does.

"Papa..."

"Yes?"

"They won 2:1 against Fiorentina."

"Great. Who scored?"

Christ, I'm making this up as I go along...

"Schillaci. Twice..."

"Schillaci never lets us down, does he?"

I don't know whether to laugh or cry. I even hate Juventus... and then it suddenly ends. He turns over and
goes to sleep.

When he wakes up in the morning, he doesn't remember any of it. When I tell him, he doesn't believe
me, and the imaginary television disappears into the
background of scenes we will never live again.

In the morning when my uncles come to relieve me, I go back home and get some sleep so I can do another night. Then my dad recovers, and the next day I go back to school and my mother stays the night. I can leave, but he is very weak and has to spend a few more days in hospital until he is allowed to come home.

We look after him. Going back to school is surreal. I worry about him, but life goes back to normal. The friends. Those wonderful friends. They help every way they can. Mirella. Fabrizio. Claudio. Andrea. Paolino. Davide. Felice. Word has spread. People come to say hi and to tell me to be strong. Our telephone never stops ringing. Relatives and neighbours turn up at home all day and in the evenings with words of encouragement, vegetables and cakes. The house of someone who is ill should never be empty. People should never be alone in their moment of need. This is the Italy that I will never forget.

Eventually even Serena calls. Time stops.

"Sorry I didn't call" I say.

"I was starting to get upset with you - the old you who never keeps his promises..."

"Don't..."

"I'm sorry about your dad..."

"Thank you."

"I hope you all get back to normal soon and – perhaps if you still feel like it, well, we have a film to watch together. Ok? Don't think you can get out of it."

I smile.

"I wouldn't miss that for the world."

"Call me when you can."

"I will."

"Speak soon then."

"Ciao."

Click.

I stare at the phone, looking embarrassed. Thank God no one can see me, but in the middle of this mayhem I really need the wonderful warm feeling that's inside me now.

A few days later my father is allowed home. I clearly remember the moment he returns home and Pongo tries to jump into the car. My father slowly gets back into his own bed after the nurses leave and it is just the three of us again after the chaos of the past few days. Then my mother goes back to the kitchen to cook, and it's just me and him. I hold his hand. He's proud and he's tough, but this has made him more gentle and he enjoys this closeness - just as I do.

"This time you were scared, eh?"

"Even Pongo was scared this time."

A beat.

"Well, Papa, when you started shouting that I hadn't set up the TV properly, I really got worried, but it was funny."

"Funny?"

"Yes, the idea that even in those circumstances, even when you were between life and death, you could tell me off - about a TV set that wasn't even there. In a way it was funny..."

"But, Alberto, tell me..."

"Yes?"

"What did I say about the TV? Did what I say make sense or was it just gibberish?"

"Well, actually, it kind of made sense. You told me to stop being wishy-washy, and to do things properly."

"Ah."

They call it a pregnant silence...

"Are you doing things properly?"

"I do try."

"Try harder. Only by doing things properly will you become a responsible adult."

"I will, Papa..."

"You know, Alberto, one thing I felt while I was in intensive care?"

"What?"

"I said to myself, Remigio, you know that you can't die. You just can't afford to die."

"Why?"

"Because I need to take care of you. You are still too young. So, I simply can't die. As simple as that."

I look at this wonderful man. Even when he was facing death, he was not thinking about himself. He was thinking about his family and about me. I just hug him and pray that in the years to come I will be able to repay this, and I think now I have. Even though I didn't learn overnight, and maybe I'm still occasionally wishy-washy.

He turns over and goes back to sleep. I kiss his forehead and go back to my room.

CHAPTER 36 - At night you find yourself alone

And it is to the emptiness of your own bedroom that you go for refuge. There, in the evening, you find yourself alone with the fear that maybe your father will die. My mother and I are reduced to just two people at the dinner table. My dad is sleeping, but sometimes he wakes up. The dog keeps vigil outside our doors. Every time we open the door he tries to come in and jump on my father's bed. Worrying about my father and whether he will live makes me suffer, and when I suffer I need to talk to someone - I can't keep it all inside.

I call Claudio and Fabrizio. No answer. I call Serena. No answer. Maybe she has her own life and her own problems. She has a party to go to. Her parents have worries. She's talking to her sister. Anyway, for whatever reason, she's not available.

I need to talk to someone though. I need to release that pain. So, my mind instantly veers towards a quick fix - however wrong. I could and should try Serena again, but I don't think she can cope with this level of stress - and I'm probably making a big mistake. So, my quick fix is to go back to Signora Vanessa.

I haven't seen or spoken to her for quite a while, and when I call, she hangs up on me. She must be very busy. I hadn't rung to tell her what had happened, because I had other, much more important, issues.

Papa is struggling. It's not easy to cope with this and lead a normal life.

Serena, in her teenage innocence, reminds me once more that the Vasco Rossi concert is in a few days. I have a million other things in my head but, like a robot, as if there were nothing more important in life, I go to my savings in the second drawer of the desk and take out the princely sum of 25,000 lira - back then a fair amount - and I buy the ticket. I feel guilty - how could I even consider going to a concert when my father almost died four days ago. But life must go on after all.

Every time something bad happens to me I have to do something to distract myself though, to forget the pain. So, it is late. Papa just had dinner in bed and went to sleep. He doesn't seem very well. I worry. It's half-past six, and he's already asleep. Very strange for him, whatever his condition. He calls from the bedroom as my mother is tidying up

"Alberto!"

"Papa?"

"Come here for a second…"

My mother and I rush in, but then we realise he just wants to talk. My mother relaxes and goes back to the kitchen. I stand next to his bed.

"You know, Alberto, I learnt one big thing this time."

"What?"

"You know it was very hard for me to accept this illness?"

"I know, Papa…"

"I was always so strong and able to sort out everything. Suddenly finding myself weak was very hard to take…"

"Of course…"

"When I realised how weak I was… that's why I said what I did… and probably hurt you so much…"

"Don't worry about it, Papa…"

"I wanted to die, because in my mind a life lived without strength wasn't worth living… But then, the last few nights… I thought of you and your mother."

Silence.

"I thought that it is important for me to live - even at half speed. Because you and your mother need me, even if I'm not the same as before. In the years to come we can have many more great moments. Like last night and the imaginary television set!"

We laugh.

"So, I see that life is about accepting and letting go. Even if it's not perfect. Even if it's not exactly 100% what you were expecting, it is always well worth living. So, this time, my son, I promise you will never again hear me wishing I could die. Because, you know, I am glad to have lived these last few months, and I look forward to the next few years. I'm sure there's so much you and I can do together..."

He turns over... and is asleep in a few seconds. Almost as if these last few words took away all his remaining energy.

Tears stream down my cheeks and I feel I have to go somewhere. I have to do something. I ask my mother for half an hour to go off on my bike to get some fresh air. It's raining outside. She complains that dinner is almost ready, but I promise to be back in an hour...

So I go out. Out into the rainy night with my Vespa, my helmet hiding my tears. But I don't go very far. I know exactly where I'm going.

It's late. It's dark. Normally I never ring her doorbell at this time of evening. I expect her husband to be back from work. But... tonight I do ring this late, and as soon as she hears me, she lets me in.

I have never been there this late, and a surprise is awaiting me. Signora Vanessa is dressed to go out tonight. I have never seen her so attractive, made up ready to go out for an evening of fun - making sure she won't go unnoticed. She is wearing one of the sexiest dresses I have ever seen on her, a purple so tight that you expect it to explode every time she moves - as slowly as a panther. I physically attack her. The tension of the last few days overwhelms me, and maybe she feels the same. I hold her close to me, I touch her, I kiss her neck, her lips - with passion and vigor. Tonight, I need to feel

258

alive. Tonight, there are not thirty years separating us. We are just two lost souls reunited who need to feel close and need each other. We kiss passionately and I lift her skirt. Touch her where I have never touched her before. She does the same. Our bodies melt. And, somehow, I feel there is a quiet music in the background of this woman, music I have not heard when I admired her from afar. Against my wildest thoughts as she opens my shirt, kisses me down and down, and slowly kneels down in front of me and... then I see it...

I don't know how, but I stop.

My body, my passion, every cell in me wants to have sex with her - wild, fast and furious. Passionate. Animalistic. Ecstatic in a way I can't begin to imagine. Everything I need for my fear, to feel I have escaped death, the misery of something now firmly in the past.

But my spirit feels this is all wrong.

Signora Vanessa looks at me for a fraction of a second as I lift her back up and hug her - panting and sweating. She is panting more than me and seems very, very confused. Maybe this is the first time something like this has happened to her - a man running away from her embrace.

She looks me in the eye. There is not much to say. I just about manage to get hold of my thoughts. Better late than never.

"What happened?"

"Maybe I just started seeing more black and white…"

She smiles. Silence around us. Neither of us knows what's left to say.

"I am tired of grey."

We've barely had time to look at each other when we hear a car stop in front of her gate. One look and we know. She laughs.

"What great timing. My husband's just arrived…"

I laugh too at the irony of it, but I have to dress, and get out of the flat as quickly as possible and go down the stairs as her burly husband comes up. Signora Vanessa and I look at each other, not quite sure about what just happened and what it means, but there's no time to think. Maybe it's better this way.

Our last minute together is the most poignant. I leave as I see her fixing her makeup as if nothing had happened. Getting ready to go out. Inside I'm smiling. I know I made the right decision. After all, I want to be able to look Serena in the eye tomorrow. Whatever happens. I walk down the three flights of stairs, my heart beating faster and faster.

I meet her husband on the stairs. Unbelievable. The most adrenaline I've ever had in my life. I'm sure her perfume is still on me, and I feel him looking at me suspiciously. I am sure she will be able to invent some story before they go out for a wonderful meal together.

Maybe tonight they will make love afterwards - and maybe she will think of me and maybe she won't. But I won't think of her. I have more important things to do. I have to learn to be black and white and chase the light - just like my dad said.

A million thoughts cross my mind as I ride the Vespa back across the silent village and I pass Serena's house, and it is there that it happens. I see the black convertible again, and I see them clearly as my little cone of light approaches the side road. I see Luca and Serena outside her door. Him with his arm against the wall as if he owns the place. She is two steps behind, at the front door, two steps away but still close enough... smiling at one of his dumb jokes.

I feel this is a key moment in my life. On any other night I would have just gone home, but tonight I feel different. Tonight, it's time to do the right thing. I turn around. I go back and face the music. I want to hear what they'll say, so I drive up on my little Vespa.

I can see Luca's sarcastic smile before I even get off the Vespa, but that has no effect tonight. I'm too pumped up, too full of adrenaline. I feel wonderful.

"Buonasera."

"Oh, three of us here - what a wonderful coincidence."

"Really a coincidence, Luca, isn't it?"

Serena is loving this – and so is her sister, watching us from the window. She wouldn't miss this for anything.

"Don't you guys have homes to go to?" Serena asks.

"I just popped by to say hi and that I bought the ticket for the concert... just like you said..."

From his face, I can see Luca wasn't ready for this.

"What concert?" he asks.

"Vasco, obviously..."

He laughs...

"Vasco? Vasco's for kids..."

We both look at him. As if he's retarded.

"Luca, why don't you just go home? We kids want to talk about Vasco..."

A funny little moment. The discussion is in the middle. She can back me up or back him up. It's kind of now or never, and there she goes.

"Yes. We do. I think you really should go home to the other grown-ups like you."

I smile. She smiles. Kaboom. He's sunk. Bye-bye.

And somehow, at that incredible moment, at a quarter past seven on a rainy evening, the mythical Luca, his fancy car and his designer clothes lose their shine. I just see a confused, slightly overweight twenty-year-old hitting on a much younger girl - maybe because no one his age fancies him. He doesn't seem that mighty anymore.

Tonight, I've defeated two ghosts. Just by being there, by showing up and by confronting them. He knows it too. He may come up with something more, but tonight he's lost. As his black convertible skids off, Serena and I look at each other. And, somehow, we already feel together. Maybe that was the night that I learnt not to be wishy-washy any more.

"You okay?" she asks, "you look strange..."

"Strange?"

"A strange light in your eyes. Were you scared? That something might happen?"

"With you? Never..."

"Me neither... I just feel happy."

I hug her tight, with all my strength. I don't know where to put all this pent-up energy... so I kiss her hard on the lips. She opens her mouth... our tongues touch and little sparks appear in the sky...

Then a quiet voice from inside the house...

"Shall we just not do this at the front door please, guys..."

It's her nosy mother again. Reminding us we're just two teenagers in love, but we live in a quiet village, have proper parents and we should know how to behave. And like the good kids we are, we always pretend to listen to our parents - and then do the opposite. But ask to be forgiven the next day, like all good Catholics do. So, we separate, and with a demure kiss on the lips I leave – get back on my trusted Vespa and home in time for dinner, just as the church bells toll half-past seven. Life can be so simple sometimes. Or so I think. But tonight is not meant to be that way after all.

My father goes to bed early. I stay up to help my mother wash the dishes and tidy up. I can see that she's a bit upset, and I wonder why.

The minute she closes the door of the kitchen and lowers her voice I know this is not looking good. I worry about something serious happening to my dad, but gosh, I have absolutely no idea what she is about to say.

My mother sits down on the chair at the kitchen table opposite me and looks at her hands. Oh my God... is it going to be that bad?

"Alberto, I don't know where to start. I am so ashamed of talking about this, but I have to. I'm your mother so I have to tell you."

"Yes, Mamma..."

"I went to the gym the other day – gymnastics for older people. One of the ladies exercising with us is a younger woman - she must be in her late forties. Her name is Vanessa. Do you know her?"

I think if I could see myself in the mirror, I would see my face catch fire and my brain explode. Oh my God. How did even my mother hear?

She is very nice, very attractive and she knows it. She's very fit and comes to the gym full of airs, always dressed to the nines. As if she's going to a party - all super tight dresses and high heels. She looks like a diva from the cinema... or one of these second-rate actresses your father watches on TV late at night...

Long silence...

"She told me that she knows you... that she's met you a few times. I had no idea who she was. I thought she was someone's mother, but she doesn't have children. So, a few of the ladies were gossiping afterwards, and it sounds like she is not one of your friend's mothers at all, and I had a thought. When you go to buy bread all the time, you're going to her house, and you're visiting her almost every day..."

I'm speechless. Not sure what to say.

"Alberto?"

"Yes?"

"Don't you have anything to say?"

"What do you want me to say?"

"What are you doing with a woman who is ten years younger than me, Alberto? Are you out of your mind?"

"Mamma..."

"Alberto, the woman is married. She's known in the village for being someone not very serious. She is always after everybody else's husband. She dresses like a whore. Is this the kind of woman you want in your life?

"Mamma, she is nothing like a whore."

"Alberto. Even if she is a saint, I want you to stop seeing her immediately. You must promise me. If she is mad enough to risk her marriage for a bit of fun, it should not be with my son."

"Mamma, it's not her chasing me... it's me chasing her."

"Listen. You're eighteen. You should have some common sense, but obviously you don't, but you may be excused for being young, stupid, full of hormones or whatever. But she is forty-six ?... she really should know better than to let an eighteen-year-old into her flat when she's probably half-naked... Doesn't the woman have any shame? She could easily be your mother? Doesn't she have any self-respect?

Silence.

My mother starts crying.

266

"How could you do this to me at such a time? With all we're going through with your father, you create another problem. Another dagger in my back! How could you do this to me now, Alberto?"

"I'm sorry, Mamma. I really am."

"Do you want me to tell Papa?"

Just the thought of that makes my world collapse. My father must never find out, and just as I think that, right on cue, while my mother is crying, the kitchen door opens, and my father comes in. He even looks cute in his baby blue pajamas, half-asleep and a shadow of his former self. He sees my mother crying and immediately becomes protective. This is one of the most endearing traits in their marriage. He never ever agrees on anything with her, but if someone else attacks her, he automatically switches into protector mode - willing to fight the whole world for her honour. That's my dad. Old-fashioned values. I love him so much.

"What's going on here?"

He's walking faster and more nimbly than he has in months. Certainly since the stroke. He wraps his big arms around her and looks at me, unimpressed.

"What did you say to her? Hasn't she suffered enough?"

Then, giving her an unexpectedly tender look: "What has he done to upset you?"

267

Total silence in the room. She can't stop crying. My heart is beating as fast as a drum. Please, Mamma, don't tell him... but I haven't seen her crying like this for a long time. Then she recovers just about enough to say: "It's just the whole situation. It's all a bit too much. I was just letting off steam, and Alberto was keeping me company, weren't you, Alberto?"

I look at my mother's beautiful blue eyes full of tears. I always tease her about not giving me those beautiful eyes. A mother's love is infinite. Even now she doesn't betray me. She never would and never will. Even when she's ashamed of her only son, those blue eyes keep the secret.

"Don't worry, Papa... nothing to worry about. Just a silly old mother weeping on her only son's shoulder."

Puzzled, my father shrugs his shoulders: "If you say so..."

"Go to bed, Remo. I'll finish tidying up and join you. I'm tired."

My father shrugs again and gets a glass of water, then heads back to the bedroom, one small step at a time.

My mother finishes the dishes without another word. As she opens the kitchen door, she looks at me: "Alberto. Promise me. You must never see that woman ever again. Promise."

"I promise, Mamma. I promise."

"Don't let yourself down."

I stay in the kitchen, alone.

The light in my parents' bedroom goes off, and the whole house is dark.

Serena rings me later to see how my dad is doing. She asks about the concert too. I still don't know if I can go. It depends on my dad.

I go back to school the next morning, still not quite myself, but I have to keep up now. I can't afford to miss another year because of what's happening at home. I have to learn to be black and white and keep studying… even if I'm worried.

The following day it's Friday, the day of the concert. It's a memorable day. One of the best days of my life. I ask my dad if he feels well enough for me to go to the concert, and he seems shocked that I should even consider not going.

"Go, go. What do you think is going to happen tonight anyway? I can live a day without you, you know!"

My mother smiles in the background and says "Don't let yourself down" again.

I nod and run off to Serena's mum's car waiting for me downstairs. From our Red Panda to their Silver Mercedes. Life is looking up already.

CHAPTER 37 - Friday 22 September 1989 - STADIO COMUNALE DI TORINO

September 22nd:

• 1989 Deal barracks bombing: An IRA bomb explodes at the Royal Marine School of Music in Deal, Kent, United Kingdom, leaving 11 people dead and 22 injured.

• Torino Stadio Comunale - Vasco Rossi - 'Liberi Liberi tour'

Twenty-five thousand people in the stadium - his second concert in Torino and the end of a summer tour

by one of the most beloved Italian singers. The only one Serena and I agree on. I am more of a Guns and Roses kind of guy. She is definitely more Simple Minds.

Serena and I sit together for

the concert - one of the most successful tours in Italian music history. Quite a few of us from the village are there, but she and I only have eyes and hands for each other. The whole day is unforgettable. We picnic in front of the historic Curva Maratona, so important to Torino FC fans. My mother will take care of my dad today, but he is much better anyway so I can relax. It's Friday, and tomorrow's the weekend. Now it's late and starting to get dark. The tour is called 'Liberi Liberi', which means 'Free Free', and it is this freedom we feel on the warm autumn night.

Vasco keeps singing, hit after hit. He started at nine thirty, and it's a two-hour non-stop marathon that continues long into the night until eleven thirty. We know all the songs by heart. It's an amazing show. Towards the end we are basically exhausted and drunk with happiness.

A slow song now, called 'Una Canzone per te' (A song for you). This is our song. The one Serena and I have sung to each other in our bedrooms about a million times. We didn't expect it, so everything feels even more perfect. We sing the romantic lyrics to each other and kiss. We know. This is the moment - September 22nd will be our anniversary for the next four years.

But even this is tainted by what happened the night before.

I get home at one, drunk on happiness, adrenaline and love. The gate and the garage door are unlocked so I can go upstairs. That innocent, safe Italy of the '80s doesn't exist anymore. We started locking the garage doors about ten years later. Until then the side door was always left open, and it was my job to lock it when I was the last one home. Then when I got up to the first floor and my parents' flat, I would lock the door from the inside and that click always woke my dad up. Even today, four days after he got out of hospital, nothing has changed.

"Alberto?"

"Dormi, Papa."

"Tutto bene?"

"All good."

"Have you locked the door?"

"Locked. Buonanotte."

"Buonanotte."

And then I go to bed.

My usual dream. But I don't know if it's really a dream or my conscience speaking.

That night I have to make a choice. I have to choose whom to dream about. And tonight, I know.

I am officially with Serena. I won. I defeated all the fears and the feeling that this was never going to happen.

But now I have to make an even bigger choice.

Now I have to finish with Signora Vanessa. I know that.

I am tempted to never see her again and to just disappear into my new wholesome life and never speak to her again - until we meet again in the street maybe in a few years' time.

Or...

I decide to go there one last time, but first I write a message to the anonymous friend, which takes me the whole night, and this is what I say:

> Dear friend,
>
> Thank you for the kind message - even though it felt like a Mafia-style threat. I read between the lines, and I feel you truly care...
> I want to tell you now that I am not proud of what I have done. I am not proud of betraying the trust of a young girl who is very dear to me.
> I want to let you know that I have listened, and you have actually helped. Although the threats were a bit silly...
>
> So, dear friend, you were right, and I was wrong. And I am happy to admit it, and this is why I am writing to say this is the last time you

will see me parked here. Whoever you are, thank you for helping me make a very important decision.

All the best,
Alberto.

I park the motorbike in the usual place and leave the message on the seat where I am sure the friend will find it.

I go up. I tell her what I decided to say. Goodbye to a story that never began. We both agree and I can imagine my mother smiling in the background.

We look at each other. One last time. We hug like old friends about to embark on a long journey - maybe we will never see each other again. For a weird moment somehow, I feel I'm with a young aunt. Suddenly the age gap is clear. Something happens inside me and her sex appeal disappears. All I see is a woman wearing clothes that are inappropriate for her age and her body. No more darkness. I am ready to start this new chapter in the light. She probably is too.

I leave, and the moment is special. I sense a new life ahead as I close the door never to return.

I walk down the steps to my Vespa where I find another message from my anonymous friend. A simple blue post-it note with a smiley face.

Job done. No more wishy-washy.

My mother looks at me anxiously for another few days, but then she forgets all about it. And so, do I.

I go downstairs to walk the dog, but instead of heading towards the centre of the village and the shopping area, I go to the fields and the mountains. Nature, after all, always saves me.

CHAPTER 38 - Happily ever after?

The next day, a new phase of my life starts.

It is quite surreal, but after all these years and all those twists and turns Serena and I are actually together.

I now officially have a girlfriend who loves me. I am in love with her too, and we are a couple.

Everything takes on a different colour. Even the bus trip to school seems different, because we sit together.

I get back home with a smile on my face. Even my mother looks surprised when I don't eat huge portions of penne anymore with so much cheese that if I ate them now, I would have to go on a diet for two weeks. My father watches me from afar, amused, but I feel better than ever.

A new life starts. It's just first love, but the way it should be. We go on our first holiday together. We buy each other rings. We go off on bike trips. Car trips. We dance, and we go to our first smart restaurant together, all dressed up. We go to the cinema and the circus. We go to concerts and many, many parties. I feel good every day, in ways I never did before. This is another chapter. I am growing up into the man I want to be.

We said at the beginning that we would go back to Berlin, but we never did. We went on plenty of other trips though, all over Italy and also France, Greece and

Spain. We had a very good time and were very much in love until we realised that we weren't.

The great love story between me and Serena ended naturally four years later.

She broke up with me, and within a few months she was going out with someone else. I was alone for eighteen months, the longest time I've stayed single in my life, and then I went to London. Going to London changed my life and I never saw Serena again, but that is another chapter, and it doesn't belong here, because I want to end on an 'And they lived happily ever after' note.

CHAPTER 39 - Ten years later

Ten years later, when I am at film school and living in London, I come back to visit my parents with my fiancée, whom I met in London. In a few months she will become my wife. Ten years are a long time, and a lot of things have changed, in the world and in my family. My parents are much older. We have a new kitchen. Clinton is the President of the United States, and Hong Kong has been handed back to China. The Millennium is about to end, and we wait to dive into the 2000s. Some friends have got married. One couple have even had their first child, and it looks like I may be the next. Even Pongo is much older and can only move with difficulty, but is always my father's best friend.

Maybe on this momentous trip I want to look back into the past, so one afternoon when everybody is having a siesta, I go up to the loft looking for a box of diaries my mother had kept. That woman has never ever thrown anything away. Ever.

I read carefully, to refresh my memory, and I was taken back to those days. I think the diary I started that summer of '89 was a bit mad. Little did I imagine it would be the basis of this book. I read about all my feelings, all my thoughts, all my friends - some of whom I still see today and some who have disappeared. I read about Serena and Signora Vanessa, whom I had not thought about for years.

I close the diary. We have the village fete to go to and I am the designated driver. So, all four of us squeeze into the purple Ford Ka, renamed the sandwich by my mother, and drive to the sports centre a kilometre away.

A large marquee has been put up on the football ground for the wonderful FESTA CAMPAGNOLA. All our traditional dishes are served on paper plates, and local wine is poured into plastic cups on long picnic tables with paper tablecloths. The villagers are the chefs and waiters, the band plays traditional music, and a few elderly people dance. A wonderful atmosphere. I love bringing my parents every September.

That night is different. As I queue for food with my foreign girlfriend who was born in an Asian megalopolis and looks around at this traditional village fete as if she were in a museum, out of the corner of my eye I see a familiar shape. She is older of course, and the only woman wearing towering heels even tonight. Signora Vanessa and husband are here. She recognises me immediately and I can sense her heart skip a beat, just as mine does.

I haven't seen her in ten years and an irresistible urge to go and say hi overcomes me.

I leave my plate on the table with my mother, dad and wife-to-be and, very fittingly, say I'm going to get bread. Of all things. What a coincidence. Life is indeed funny at times. For a second, I worry that my mother may see and disapprove, but that embarrassing day at the gym is long forgotten. Or at least I hope so.

Signora Vanessa sees me coming over, smiles effusively, and finds an excuse to spend just a few moments alone with me.

"Ma buonasera"

"Buonasera..."

"How's life?" she asks. "You look well..."

"Very good. Thank you. Do I?"

"Well, the English weather hasn't transformed you into Mozzarella yet..."

"Haha! I guess we do see the sun every now and then, you know..."

She looks back at my parents' table.

"I see you have a... new flame..."

I look back as my fiancée chats amiably with my parents. No one has noticed my absence.

"The girlfriend..."

My wife-to-be is, objectively, a good-looking girl. I'm the envy of all my classmates at film school, but Signora Vanessa is not impressed, and I am not sure why I should care, but... somehow, I want to hear what she has to say...

"Well, I expected you to go out with someone a bit different…"

"Oh yes? In what way?"

She takes another look at my fiancée's understated coat and flat shoes. Her simple makeup and short hair.

"Well, someone a bit more…" She opens her coat to reveal yet again that cleavage.

"Eye-catching, if you see what I mean…"

I look at this woman in her late fifties desperately trying to hang on to the last remnants of an explosive beauty that is wilting, but her time is over. No one looks at her any more the way they used to even just ten years ago. She doesn't stop the traffic anymore. The heels are a bit lower, and even the cleavage has dropped. She has aged and it feels a bit weird to be having this conversation.

I wonder what to reply. I don't want to say anything that will upset her. But although I feel I should say something, it's not meant to be. Suddenly my fiancée appears and picks up some bread, but she doesn't even look at the old lady in front of me. She just says hello politely and drags me away without a second look, never imagining that this same woman ten years before tormented me for an entire, hot, unforgettable summer.

But that is all over.

I will never see her again, and the next chapter of my life is about to begin.

Epilogue

NOVEMBER 9th, 1989

Cold War and Fall of the Berlin Wall: Günter Schabowski accidentally states in a live broadcast press conference that new rules for travelling from East Germany to West Germany will be put in effect "immediately". East Germany opens checkpoints in the Berlin Wall, allowing its citizens to travel freely to West Germany for the first time in decades (November 17 celebrates Germans tearing the wall down).

My father is watching the news again and I am sitting next to him at the living room table. My mother is pottering around as always: our small family of three battling a world changing too fast for my beloved father.

He stands up in the middle of lunch and heads solemnly for his bedroom. As he walks away, I listen to the news and the celebrations from Berlin. Families reunited. Beautiful stories of unity and hope. Yet my father is in his bedroom opening his lacquered storage box - the one with all the documents.

He takes out the piece of the Wall that Serena brought from Berlin, and he takes out his precious Membership Card of the Italian Communist party (PCI). He has been proud to be a PCI member since the 1950s, when the party was founded in Italy. It's the largest Communist party in Western Europe.

My dad takes the wall out of its plastic case and gently lays the PCI card on the fragments of brick that came all the way from Germany - a Germany he never set foot in again after the end of the war.

He takes one of the matches my mother uses to light the flames on the gas hob. The match sparks and flashes, and a small orange flame lights up his face.

He sets fire to his PCI card and lets it burn slowly on the Berlin Wall.

We all watch as the paper card blackens and turns to ashes...

Then the flame dies.

My dad puts the plastic case back on the wall and the ashes.

"That's it, my son. From today I'm not a communist anymore. It's time to move on. Capitalism has won, but we will never be defeated. Good night."

He goes to bed and sleeps soundly — and never looks at that card again.

THE END
- *PAX MERCEIRO AND GENERAL 7* -

Remember young people:

Everything is possible if you put your heart into it. Chase the light, don't fall for darkness. Life is wonderful – if you just take time to discover who you truly are.

TO CLAUDIO SCAVAZZA, one of my few brothers in life - DJ Bombato. (b. 24 - 4 1970 - d. 4 - 3 - 2019)

Gone too soon but never forgotten

CIAO BABBEO XX

1989 - Day by day

[Source Wikipedia]

January

- January 2 – Prime Minister Ranasinghe Premadasa takes office as the third President of Sri Lanka.
- January 4 – Gulf of Sidra incident (1989): Two Libyan MiG-23 "Floggers" are engaged and shot down by 2 US Navy F-14 Tomcats.
- January 7 – Hirohito dies, and Akihito is enthroned as the 125th Emperor of Japan immediately, followed by the change in the era name from Showa to Heisei on the following day.
- January 8 – Kegworth air disaster: A British Midland Boeing 737 crashes on approach to East Midlands Airport, leaving 47 dead.
- January 10 – In accordance with United Nations Security Council Resolution 626 and the New York Accords, Cuban troops begin withdrawing from Angola.
- January 11 - Outgoing U.S. President Ronald Reagan delivers his farewell address to the nation after eight years in office.
- The Lexus and Infiniti luxury car brands are launched at the North American International Auto Show in Detroit with the unveiling of the 1990 Lexus LS and Infiniti Q45 sedans.
- January 15 - Thirty-five European nations, meeting in Vienna, agree to strengthen human rights and improve East-West trade.

- "Palach Week": A pro-democracy demonstration in Prague is attacked by the police.[4]
- January 17 – Stockton schoolyard shooting: Patrick Edward Purdy kills five children, wounds thirty and then shoots himself in Stockton, California.
- January 18 - The Polish United Workers' Party votes to legalise Solidarity.
- Ante Marković succeeds Branko Mikulić as Prime Minister of Yugoslavia.
- January 20 – George H. W. Bush is sworn in as the 41st President of the United States.
- January 23 – A powerful earthquake in the Tajik Soviet Socialist Republic kills around 275 people.
- January 23–24 – Armed civilian leftists briefly attack and occupy an Argentinian army base near Buenos Aires.
- January 24 – Florida executes Ted Bundy by electric chair for the murders of young women.
- January 29 – The British children's television show Thomas & Friends, begins airing in the United States with the series premiere of Shining Time Station on PBS.
- January 30 – Prime Minister of Canada Brian Mulroney shuffles his cabinet, appointing six new ministers and reassigning the responsibilities of nineteen others.

February

- February 1 – Joan Kirner becomes Victoria's first female Deputy Premier, after the resignation of Robert Fordham over the VEDC (Victorian Economic Development Co-operation) Crisis.
- February 2 - Soviet–Afghan War: The last Soviet Union armoured column leaves Kabul, ending nine years of military occupation since 1979.
- Carlos Andrés Pérez takes office as President of Venezuela.
- Satellite television service Sky Television plc is launched in Europe.
- February 3 - A military coup overthrows Alfredo Stroessner, dictator of Paraguay since 1954.
- After a stroke, State President of South Africa P. W. Botha resigns as Leader of the National Party.
- February 5 – Eurosport, a multiple-language sports broadcasting station in Europe opens in Issy-les-Moulineaux, Ile de France, France.
- February 6 – The Government of the People's Republic of Poland holds formal talks with representatives of the Solidarity movement for the first time since 1981.
- February 7 - The People's National Party, led by Michael Manley, wins the 1989 Jamaican general election.
- The Los Angeles City Council bans the sale or possession of semi-automatic firearms.
- February 10 - Ron Brown is elected as Chairman of the Democratic National Committee, becom-

ing the first African American to lead a major United States political party.

- U.S. President Bush meets Canadian Prime Minister Brian Mulroney in Ottawa, laying the groundwork for the Acid Rain Treaty of 1991.
- February 11 – Barbara Harris is the first woman consecrated as a bishop of the Episcopal Church in the United States of America (and also the first woman to become a bishop in the worldwide Anglican Communion).
- February 14 - US$470,000,000 damages to the Indian Government for the 1984 Bhopal disaster.
- The Satanic Verses controversy: Ayatollah Ruhollah Khomeini, Supreme Leader of Iran (d. June 3), issues a fatwa calling for the death of Indian-born British author Salman Rushdie and his publishers for issuing the novel The Satanic Verses (1988).
- The first of 24 Global Positioning System satellites is placed into orbit.
- February 15 - Soviet–Afghan War: The Soviet Union announces that all of its troops have left Afghanistan.
- Following a campaign that saw over 1,000 people killed in massive campaign-related violence, the United National Party wins the Sri Lankan parliamentary election.
- February 16 – Pan Am Flight 103: Investigators announce that the cause of the crash was a bomb hidden inside a radio-cassette player.
- February 17 - The Arab Maghreb Union (AMU) is formed.

- South African police raid the home of Winnie Mandela and arrest four of her bodyguards.
- February 20 – In Canada's Yukon Territory, the ruling New Democrats narrowly maintain control of the Yukon Legislative Assembly, winning 9 seats vs. the Progressive Conservative Party's 7.
- February 23 – After protracted testimony, the U.S. Senate Armed Services Committee rejects, 11–9, President Bush's nomination of John Tower for Secretary of Defense.
- February 23–27 – U.S. President Bush visits Japan, China, and South Korea, attending the funeral of Hirohito and then meeting with China's Deng Xiaoping and South Korea's Roh Tae-woo.
- February 24 - The funeral of Hirohito is attended by representatives of 160 nations.
- The Satanic Verses controversy: Iran places a $3,000,000 bounty on the head of The Satanic Verses author Salman Rushdie.
- Singing Revolution: After 44 years, the Estonian flag is raised at the Pikk Hermann tower in Tallinn.
- United Airlines Flight 811, a Boeing 747, suffers uncontrolled decompression after leaving Honolulu International Airport, nine passengers are sucked out of the cabin to their deaths.
- February 27 – Venezuela is rocked by the Caracazo, a wave of protests and looting.
- Mass demonstration at State TV HQ
- The Exxon Valdez

March

Poland begins to liberalize its currency exchange in a move towards capitalism.[5]

- March 1 - The Berne Convention, an international treaty on copyrights, is ratified by the United States.

- A curfew is imposed in Kosovo, where protests continue over the alleged intimidation of the Serb minority.
- The Politieke Partij Radicalen, Pacifistisch Socialistische Partij, Communistische Partij Nederland and the Evangelical People's Partyamalgamate to form the Dutch political party GroenLinks (GL, GreenLeft).
- After 74 years, Iceland ends its prohibition on beer; celebrated since as bjórdagur or beer day.
- March 2 – Twelve European Community nations agree to ban the production of all chlorofluorocarbons (CFCs) by the end of the century.
- March 3 – Jammu Siltavuori abducts and murders two eight-year-old girls in the Myllypuro suburb of Helsinki, Finland.
- March 4 - Time Inc. and Warner Communications announce plans for a merger, forming Time Warner.
- The Purley station rail crash in London leaves five people dead and 94 injured.
- The first ACT (Australian Capital Territory) elections are held.
- March 7 – Iran breaks off diplomatic relations with the United Kingdom over Salman Rushdie's The Satanic Verses.

- March 9 – Revolutions of 1989: The Soviet Union submits to the jurisdiction of the World Court.
- March 13 - A geomagnetic storm causes the collapse of the Hydro-Québec power grid. 6,000,000 people are left without power for nine hours. Some areas in the northeastern U.S. and in Sweden also lose power, and aurorae are seen as far as Texas.
- Tim Berners-Lee produces the proposal document that will become the blueprint for the World Wide Web.[6]
- March 14 - Gun control: U.S. President George H. W. Bush bans the importation of certain guns deemed to be classed as assault weapons into the United States.
- Christian General Michel Aoun declares a "War of Liberation" to rid Lebanon of Syrian forces and their allies.
- March 15 - Israel hands over Taba to Egypt, ending a seven-year territorial dispute.
- Mass demonstrations in Hungary, demanding democracy.
- March 16 – The Central Committee of the Communist Party of the Soviet Union approves agricultural reforms allowing farmers the right to lease state-owned farms for life.
- March 17 - The Civic Tower of Pavia, built in the eleventh century, collapses.
- Alfredo Cristiani is elected President of El Salvador.

- March 20 – Australian Prime Minister Bob Hawke weeps on national television as he admits marital infidelity.
- March 22 - Clint Malarchuk of the NHL Buffalo Sabres suffers an almost fatal injury when another player accidentally slits his throat.
- Asteroid 4581 Asclepius approaches the Earth at a distance of 700,000 kilometres (430,000 mi).
- March 23 – Stanley Pons and Martin Fleischmann announce that they have achieved cold fusion at the University of Utah.
- March 23–28 – The Socialist Republic of Serbia passes constitutional changes revoking the autonomy of the Socialist Autonomous Province of Kosovo, triggering six days of rioting by the Albanian majority, during which at least 29 people are killed.
- March 24 – Exxon Valdez oil spill: In Alaska's Prince William Sound, the Exxon Valdez spills 240,000 barrels (38,000 m3) of oil after running aground.
- March 26 – The first contested elections for the Soviet parliament, Congress of People's Deputies, result in losses for the Communist Party.
- March 29 – The 61st Academy Awards are held at the Shrine Auditorium in Los Angeles, with Rain Man winning Best Picture.

April

- The death of Hu Yaobang sparks the beginning of the Tiananmen Square protests.
- April 1 – Margaret Thatcher's new local government tax, the Poll tax, is introduced in Scotland. It would be introduced in England & Wales the following year.
- April 2 - In South-West Africa, fighting erupts between SWAPO insurgents and the Southwest African Police on the day that a ceasefire was supposed to end the South African Border War according to United Nations Security Council Resolution 435. By April 6, nearly 300 people are killed.
- April 4 - A failed coup attempt against Prosper Avril, President of Haiti, leads to a standoff between mutinous troops and the government which ends on April 10, with the government regaining control of the country.
- In Brussels, Belgium, NATO celebrates its fortieth anniversary.
- April 5 – The Polish Government and the Solidarity trade union sign an agreement restoring Solidarity to legal status and agreeing to hold democratic elections on June 1.
- April 6 – National Safety Council of Australia chief executive John Friedrich is arrested after defrauding investors to the tune of $235,000,000.
- April 7 – The Soviet submarine K-278 Komsomolets sinks in the Barents Sea, killing 41.

- April 9 - Tbilisi massacre: Georgian demonstrators are massacred by Red Army soldiers in Tbilisi's central square during a peaceful rally; 20 citizens are killed, many injured.
- A dispute over grazing rights leads to the beginning of the Mauritania–Senegal Border War.
- April 14 – The U.S. government seizes the Irvine, California, Lincoln Savings and Loan Association; Charles Keating (for whom the Keating Five were named) eventually goes to jail, as part of the massive 1980s savings and loan crisis which cost U.S. taxpayers nearly $200,000,000 in bailouts, and many people their life savings.[7]
- April 15 - The death of Hu Yaobang sparks the beginning of the Tiananmen Square protests of 1989.
- The Hillsborough disaster, one of the biggest tragedies in European football, claims the life of 96 Liverpool F.C. supporters.
- April 17 – Poland, Solidarity is once again legalized and allowed to participate in semi-free elections on June 4.
- April 19 - Trisha Meili is attacked whilst jogging in New York City's Central Park; as her identity remains secret for years, she is referred to as the "Central Park Jogger."
- A gun turret explodes on the U.S. battleship Iowa, killing 47 crew members.
- April 20 – NATO debates modernising short range missiles; although the US and UK are in favour, West German Chancellor Helmut Kohl obtains a concession deferring a decision.

- April 21 – Students from Beijing, Shanghai, Xi'an, and Nanjing begin protesting in Tiananmen Square.
- April 23 - Zaid al-Rifai resigns as Prime Minister of Jordan in the wake of riots over government-imposed price hikes that began on April 18.
- April 25 - Noboru Takeshita resigns as Prime Minister of Japan in the wake of a stock-trading scandal.
- The term of Baginda Almutawakkil Alallah Sultan Iskandar Al-Haj ibni Almarhum Sultan Ismail as the 8th Yang di-Pertuan Agong of Malaysia ends.
- Motorola introduces the Motorola MicroTAC Personal Cellular Telephone, then the world's smallest mobile phone.
- April 26 - Sultan Azlan Muhibbudin Shah ibni Almarhum Sultan Yusuff Izzudin Shah Ghafarullahu-lahu, Sultan of Perak, becomes the 9th Yang di-Pertuan Agong of Malaysia.
- Zaid ibn Shaker succeeds Zaid al-Rifai as Prime Minister of Jordan.
- The Daulatpur–Saturia tornado, the deadliest tornado ever recorded, kills an estimated 1,300 people in the Dhaka Division of Bangladesh.
- April 27 – A major demonstration occurs in Beijing, as part of the Tiananmen Square protests.[4]
- Transhumanism – Genetic modification of adult human beings is tried for the first time, a gene tagging trial.[8]

- The Soviet Union issues its first Visa card in a step to digitalize their banking system.[9]

May

- May 1 - Andrés Rodríguez, who had seized power and declared himself President of Paraguay during a military coup in February, wins a landslide victory at a general election marked by charges of fraud.
- Disney-MGM Studios at Walt Disney World opens to the public for the first time.
- May 2 - The first crack in the Iron Curtain: Hungary dismantles 150 miles (240 km) of barbed wire fencing along the border with Austria.
- The coalition government of Prime Minister of the Netherlands Ruud Lubbers collapses in a dispute about a pollution cleanup plan.
- May 3 – Cold War – Perestroika – The first McDonald's restaurant in the USSR begins construction in Moscow. It will open on 31 January 1990.[10]
- May 4 – Oliver North convicted on charges related to the Iran–Contra affair. His conviction was thrown out on appeal in 1991 because of his immunised testimony.
- May 9 – Andrew Peacock deposes John Howard as Federal Opposition Leader of Australia.
- May 10 – The government of President of Panama Manuel Noriega declares void the result of the May 7 presidential election, which Noriega had lost to Guillermo Endara.

- May 11 - President Bush orders 1,900 U.S. troops to Panama to protect Americans there.
- The ACT (Australian Capital Territory) Legislative Assembly meets for the first time.
- May 14 - Mikhail Gorbachev visits China, the first Soviet leader to do so since Nikita Khrushchev in the 1960s.
- Carlos Menem wins the Argentine presidential election.
- May 15 – Australia's first private tertiary institution, Bond University, opens on the Gold Coast.
- May 16 – Ethiopia Coup Attempt: Senior military officers' stage a coup attempt in Ethiopia hours after President Mengistu Haile Mariam leaves on a visit to East Germany.
- May 17 – More than 1,000,000 Chinese protestors march through Beijing demanding greater democracy.
- May 19, 1989 - Ürümqi unrest: Uyghur and Hui Muslim protesters riot in front of the government building in Ürümqi, China.
- Tiananmen Square protests of 1989: Zhao Ziyang meets the demonstrators in Tiananmen Square.
- Ciriaco De Mita resigns as Prime Minister of Italy.
- May 20 – Tiananmen Square protests of 1989: The Chinese government declares martial law in Beijing.
- May 22 – The Nordland Days in Leningrad region (Leningrad Oblast) open.

- May 29 - Amid food riots and looting set off by inflation, the Government of Argentina declares a nationwide state of siege.
- Boris Yeltsin gains a seat on the Supreme Soviet of the Soviet Union.
- Tiananmen Square protests of 1989: The 10-metre (33 ft) high Goddess of Democracy statue is unveiled in Tiananmen Square by student demonstrators.
- NATO agrees to talks with the Soviet Union on reducing the number of short-range nuclear weapons in Europe.
- An attempted assassination of Miguel Maza Marquez, director of the Departamento Administrativo de Seguridad (DAS) in Bogotá, Colombia is committed by members of the Medellín Cartel, who kill four and injure 37.
- May 31 – Six members of the guerrilla group Revolutionary Movement Tupac Amaru (MRTA) of Peru, shoot dead eight transsexuals, in the city of Tarapoto.[11]

June

People's Liberation Army were to drive away students in Tiananmen Square.
- June 1–10 – Pope John Paul II visits Norway, Iceland, Finland, Denmark, and Sweden.
- June 2 – Sōsuke Uno succeeds Noboru Takeshita as Prime Minister of Japan.
- June 3 - Fighting breaks out in the Uzbek Soviet Socialist Republic between ethnic Uzbeks and

the Turkish minority; more than 100 people are killed by June 15.

- The world's first HDTV broadcasts commence in Japan, in analogue.[12]
- June 4 - The Tiananmen Square crackdown takes place in Beijing on the army's approach to the square, and the final stand-off in the square is covered live on television.
- Solidarity's victory in Polish elections is the first of many anti-communist revolutions in Central and Eastern Europe in 1989.
- Ufa train disaster: A natural gas explosion near Ufa, Russia kills 645 as two trains passing each other throw sparks near a leaky pipeline.
- June 5 – An unknown Chinese protestor, "Tank Man", stands in front of a column of military tanks on Chang'an Avenue in Beijing, temporarily halting them, an incident which achieves iconic status internationally through images taken by Western photographers.
- June 6 – The Ayatollah Khomeini's first funeral is aborted by officials after a large crowd storms the funeral procession, nearly destroying Khomeini's wooden casket in order to get a last glimpse of his body. At one point, Khomeini's body almost falls to the ground, as the crowd attempt to grab pieces of the death shroud.[13]
- June 7 – Surinam Airways Flight 764 crashes in Paramaribo, Suriname; killing 176.
- June 13 – The wreck of the German battleship Bismarck, which was sunk in 1941, is located 600 miles (970 km) west of Brest, France.

- June 15 – At the 1989 Irish general election, Fianna Fáil, led by Taoiseach Charles Haughey, fails to win a majority.
- June 16 – A crowd of 250,000 gathers at Heroes Square in Budapest for the historic reburial of Imre Nagy, the former Hungarian Prime Minister who had been executed in 1958.
- June 18 – In the first Greek legislative election of the year, the Panhellenic Socialist Movement, led by Prime Minister of Greece Andreas Papandreou, loses control of the Hellenic Parliament, leading to Papandreou's resignation on July 2.
- June 24 – Jiang Zemin becomes General Secretary of the Communist Party of China.
- June 30 – A military coup led by Omar al-Bashir ousts the civilian government of Prime Minister of Sudan Sadiq al-Mahdi.

July

- July 2 – Andreas Papandreou, Prime Minister of Greece resigns; a new government is formed under Tzannis Tzannetakis.
- The television sitcom Seinfeld premieres.
- July 6 – The Tel Aviv–Jerusalem bus 405 suicide attack, the first Palestinian suicide attack on Israel, takes place.
- July 9 – 12 – U.S. President George H. W. Bush travels to Poland and Hungary, pushing for U.S. economic aid and investment.
- Voice actor Mel Blanc, comedian, singer and radio personality, dubbed The Man of a Thousand

Voices, of many cartoon characters dies at the Cedars-Sinai Medical Centre from heart disease at the age of 81 (Born 1908).

- July 12 – In the Republic of Ireland, the Taoiseach Charles Haughey returns to power after Fianna Fáil forms a coalition with the Progressive Democrats.
- July 19 - The National Assembly of the Republic of Poland elects Wojciech Jaruzelski to the new and powerful post of President of Poland.
- United Airlines Flight 232 (Douglas DC-10) crashes in Sioux City, Iowa, killing 112; 184 on board survive.
- July 21 – A total blockade of Armenia and NKAO by Azerbaijan begins.
- July 23 - Japan's ruling Liberal Democratic Party loses control of the House of Councillors, the LDP's worst electoral showing in 34 years, leading to Prime Minister Uno announcing he will resign to take responsibility for the result.
- Giulio Andreotti takes office as Prime Minister of Italy.
- July 31 - In Lebanon, Hezbollah announces that it has hanged U.S. Marine Lt. Col. William R. Higgins in retaliation for Israel's July 28 kidnapping of Hezbollah leader Abdel Karim Obeid. The same day, the United Nations Security Council passes United Nations Security Council Resolution 638, condemning the taking of hostages by both sides in the conflict.
- Nintendo releases the Game Boy portable video game system in North America.

August

Voyager 2 at Neptune
- August 2 – Pakistan is readmitted to the Commonwealth of Nations after leaving it in 1972.
- August 5 – Jaime Paz Zamora is elected President of Bolivia, taking office the next day.
- August 7 - U.S. Congressman Mickey Leland (D-TX) and fifteen others die in a plane crash in Ethiopia.
- The presidents of five Central American countries agree that the U.S.-backed contras fighting the government of Nicaragua should be disbanded and evicted from their bases in Honduras by December 5.
- August 8 - Prime Minister of New Zealand David Lange resigns for health reasons and is replaced by Geoffrey Palmer.
- STS-28: Space Shuttle Columbia takes off on a secret five-day military mission.
- August 9 - Toshiki Kaifu becomes Prime Minister of Japan.
- The asteroid 4769 Castalia is the first asteroid directly imaged by radar from Arecibo Observatory.
- A measure to rescue the savings and loan industry is signed into law by President Bush, launching the largest federal rescue to date.
- August 13 – A hot air balloon accident near Alice Springs, Australia kills thirteen people.
- August 15 - P.W. Botha resigns as State President of South Africa.[15]

- F. W. de Klerk becomes the seventh and final State President of South Africa.[15]
- August 18 – Leading presidential hopeful Luis Carlos Galán is assassinated near Bogotá, Colombia.
- August 19 - Polish president Wojciech Jaruzelski nominates Solidarity activist Tadeusz Mazowiecki to be Prime Minister, the first non-Communist in power in 42 years.
- The Pan-European Picnic, a peace demonstration, is held at the Austro-Hungarian border.
- August 19–21 – In response to the murder of a judge, a provincial police chief, and presidential candidate Galán, the authorities of Colombia arrest 11,000 suspected Colombian drug traffickers.
- August 20 - In Beverly Hills, California, Lyle and Erik Menendez shoot their wealthy parents to death in the family's den.
- Fifty-one people die when the Marchioness pleasure boat collides with a barge on the River Thames adjacent to Southwark Bridge.
- August 21 – The 21st anniversary of the crushing of the Prague Spring is commemorated by a demonstration in the city.[4]
- August 23 - Singing Revolution: Two million indigenous people of Estonian, LaTVian and Lithuanian SSRs join hands to demand freedom and independence from Soviet occupation, forming an uninterrupted 600 km human chain called the Baltic Way.
- Hungary removes border restrictions with Austria.

- All of Australia's 1,645 domestic airline pilots resign over an airline's move to sack and sue them over a dispute.
- August 23 – Yusef Hawkins is shot in the Bensonhurst section of Brooklyn, New York, sparking racial tensions between African Americans and Italian Americans.
- August 24 - Colombia's cocaine traffickers declare "total and absolute war" against the government and begin a series of bombings and arson attacks.
- Voyager 2 makes its closest approach to Neptune.
- Tadeusz Mazowiecki of Solidarity is elected Prime Minister of Poland.[4]
- August 25 – Voyager 2 passes the planet Neptune and its moon Triton.
- August 31 – In the aftermath of the Chadian–Libyan conflict of 1978–87, representatives of Libya and Chad agree to let the International Court of Justice determine ownership of the Aouzou Strip, which had been occupied by Libya since 1973.

September

- At the 1989 Dutch general election, the Christian Democratic Appeal, led by Ruud Lubbers wins 54 seats, and is ultimately able to form a government on November 7 after entering into coalition with the Labour Party.
- September 8 – Partnair Flight 394 flies past an F-16 Fighting Falcon on its way home, then the

Convair 580 rolls upside down and falls in the North Sea.

- September 10–11 – Norway's ruling Labour Party loses eight seats in the parliamentary elections, its worst showing since 1945.
- September 14 - An agreement of co-operation between Leningrad Oblast (Russia) and Nordland County (Norway) is signed in Leningrad, by Chairmen Lev Kojkolainen and Sigbjørn Eriksen.
- Standard Gravure shooting: Joseph T. Wesbecker, a pressman on disability for mental illness, entered his former workplace and killed eight people and injured twelve before committing suicide after a history of suicidal ideation.
- September 17–22 – Hurricane Hugo devastates the Caribbean and the southeastern United States, causing at least 71 deaths and $8,000,000,000 in damages.
- September 19 - The Catholic Church calls for removal of the Carmelite convent located near the former Auschwitz concentration camp, whose presence had offended some Jewish leaders.
- UTA Flight 772 explodes over Niger, killing all 171 people on board (the Islamic Jihad Organization claims responsibility).
- Burkinabé ministers Jean-Baptiste Boukary Lingani and Henri Zongo executed following their arrest the previous day.
- September 20 – F. W. de Klerk is sworn in as the seventh and last State President of South Africa.[15]

- Doe v. University of Michigan: A Michigan court rules against the hate speech law at the University of Michigan, claiming it unconstitutional.[16]
- September 26 – Vietnam announces that it has withdrawn the last of its troops from the State of Cambodia, ending an eleven-year occupation.
- September 30 - Nearly 7,000 East Germans who had come to Prague on special refugee trains are allowed to leave for the West.
- The Senegambia Confederation is dissolved over border disagreements.

October

- The Phillips Disaster
- October – Cold War – Perestroika – Nathan's Famous opens a hot dog stand in Moscow.[17]
- October 1 – Civil union between partners in a same-sex relationship becomes legal in Denmark under a law enacted on June 7, the world's first such legislation.[18][19]
- October 3 - A coup attempt is foiled by Manuel Noriega, military leader of Panama.
- The government of East Germany closes the country's border with Czechoslovakia to prevent further emigration to the West.[4]
- October 5 – The Dalai Lama wins the Nobel Peace Prize.
- October 7 - The communist Hungarian Socialist Workers' Party votes to reorganise itself as a socialist party, to be named the Hungarian Socialist Party.

- The first mass demonstration against the Communist regime in the GDR began in Plauen, East Germany, on 7 October 1989 and it was the beginning of a series of mass demonstrations in the whole GDR which ultimately led to the reunification of Germany in 1990.
- October 9 - An official news agency in the Soviet Union reports the landing of a UFO in Voronezh.
- In Leipzig, East Germany, protesters demand the legalisation of opposition groups and democratic reforms.
- October 13 - Friday the 13th mini crash: The Dow Jones Industrial Average plunges 190.58 points, or 6.91 percent, to close at 2,569.26, most likely after the junk bond market collapses.
- Gro Harlem Brundtland, leader of the Labour Party, resigns as Prime Minister of Norway. She is succeeded by Jan P. Syse, Leader of the Conservative Party, on October 16.
- October 15 – Walter Sisulu is released from prison in South Africa.[4]
- October 17 – The 6.9 Mw Loma Prieta earthquake shakes the San Francisco Bay Area and the Central Coast with a maximother Mercalli intensity of IX (Violent). Sixty-three people were killed, and the 1989 World Series is postponed for ten days as a result of the earthquake.
- October 18 - The Communist leader of East Germany, Erich Honecker, is forced to step down as leader of the country after a series of health problems and is succeeded by Egon Krenz.

- The National Assembly of Hungary votes to restore multi-party democracy.
- NASA launches the unmanned Galileo orbiter on a mission to study the planet Jupiter, via Atlantis mission STS-34.
- October 19 - The Guildford Four are freed after fourteen years.
- The Wonders of Life pavilion opens at Epcot in Walt Disney World, Florida.
- October 21 – The Heads of Government of the Commonwealth of Nations issue the Langkawi Declaration on the Environment, making environmental sustainability one of the Commonwealth's main priorities.
- October 23 - The Hungarian Republic is officially declared by President Mátyás Szűrös (replacing the Hungarian People's Republic), exactly 33 years after the Hungarian Revolution of 1956.
- The Phillips Disaster in Pasadena, Texas kills 23 and injures 314 others.
- October 28 – United States Flag Protection Act takes effect. Mass protests in Seattle and New York City
- October 30 – Shawn Eichman, Dave Blalock, Dread Scott, and Joey Johnson burn American flags on steps of U.S. Capitol Building to protest Flag Protection Act [20]
- October 31 - The Grand National Assembly of Turkey elects Prime Minister Turgut Özal as the eighth President of Turkey.
- Half a million people demonstrate in the East German city of Leipzig.[4]

November

- Germans standing on top of the Berlin Wall
- A peaceful demonstration in Prague during the Velvet Revolution.
- November – First commercial dial-up Internet connection in North America is made, by The World STD. [21]
- November 1 - The President of Nicaragua ends a ceasefire with U.S.-backed contras that had been in effect since April 1988.
- The border between East Germany and Czechoslovakia is reopened.[4]
- November 3 – East German refugees arrive at the West German town of Hof after being allowed through Czechoslovakia.[4]
- November 4 – Typhoon Gay devastates Thailand's Chumphon Province.
- November 6 – The Asia-Pacific Economic Cooperation (APEC) is founded.
- November 7 - Douglas Wilder wins the Virginia govenatorial race, becoming the first elected African American Governor in the United States.
- David Dinkins becomes the first African American mayor of New York City.
- Cold War: The Communist government of East Germany resigns, although SED leader Egon Krenz remains as head of state.
- November 9 - Cold War and Fall of the Berlin Wall: Günter Schabowski accidentally states in a live broadcast press conference that new rules for travelling from East Germany to West Germany will be put in effect "immediately". East

Germany opens checkpoints in the Berlin Wall, allowing its citizens to travel freely to West Germany for the first time in decades (November 17 celebrates Germans tearing the wall down).

- Yıldırım Akbulut of ANAP forms the new government of Turkey (47th government).
- November 10
- After 45 years of Communist rule in Bulgaria, Bulgarian Communist Party leader Todor Zhivkov is replaced by Foreign Minister Petar Mladenov, who changes the party's name to the Bulgarian Socialist Party.
- Gaby Kennard becomes the first Australian woman to fly solo around the world.
- CKO (a Canadian national all-news radio network) suddenly terminates all broadcasting during the newscast at noon (Eastern time), due to financial losses (the station began broadcasting on July 1, 1977).
- November 12 – Brazil holds its first free presidential election since 1960. This marks the first time that all Ibero-American nations, except Cuba, have elected constitutional governments simultaneously.
- November 13 – Hans-Adam II becomes Prince of Liechtenstein on the death of his father, Prince Franz Joseph II.
- November 14 – Elections are held in Namibia, leading to a victory for the SouthWest Africa People's Organisation.[4]

- November 15 - Lech Wałęsa, leader of Poland's Solidarity movement, addresses a Joint session of the United States Congress.
- Brazil holds the first round of its first free election in 29 years; Fernando Collor de Mello and Luiz Inácio Lula da Silva advance to the second round, to be held the following month.
- November 16 - Six Jesuit priests are murdered by U.S. trained Salvadoran soldiers.
- The first American cosmetics shop, an Estée Lauder outlet, opens in Moscow.[17]
- South African President F. W. de Klerk announces the scrapping of the Separate Amenities Act.
- UNESCO adopts the Seville Statement on Violence at the 25th session of its General Conference.
- November 17 – Cold War – Velvet Revolution: A peaceful student demonstration in Prague, Czechoslovakia, is severely beaten back by riot police. This sparks a revolution aimed at overthrowing the Communist government (it succeeds on December 29).
- November 20 – Cold War – Velvet Revolution: The number of peaceful protesters assembled in Prague, Czechoslovakia, swells from 200,000 the day before to an estimated half-million.
- November 21 – The Members of the Constituent Assembly of Namibia begin to draft the Constitution of Namibia, which will be the constitution of the newly independent Namibia.

- November 22 – In West Beirut, a bomb explodes near the motorcade of Lebanese President René Moawad, killing him.
- November 24 – Following a week of demonstrations demanding free elections and other reforms, General Secretary Miloš Jakeš and other leaders of the Communist Party of Czechoslovakia resign. Jakeš is replaced by Karel Urbánek.
- November 26 – Uruguayan general election, 1989: Luis Alberto Lacalle is elected President of Uruguay.
- November 27 – Colombian domestic passenger flight Avianca Flight 203 is bombed by the Medellín drug cartel in an (unsuccessful) attempt to kill presidential candidate for the 1990 elections César Gaviria Trujillo.
- November 28 – Cold War – Velvet Revolution: The Communist Party of Czechoslovakia announces they will give up their monopoly on political power (elections held in December bring the first non-Communist government to Czechoslovakia in more than forty years).
- November 29 – Rajiv Gandhi resigns as Prime Minister of India after his party, the Indian National Congress, loses about half of its seats at the 1989 Indian general election.
- November 30 – Deutsche Bank board member Alfred Herrhausen is killed by a bomb (the Red Army Faction claims responsibility for the murder).

December

- Flames engulf a building following the United States invasion of Panama.

- December 1 - In a meeting with Pope John Paul II, General Secretary of the Soviet Union Mikhail Gorbachev pledges greater religious freedom for citizens of the Soviet Union.

- Cold War: East Germany's parliament abolishes the constitutional provision granting the Communist-dominated SED its monopoly on power. Egon Krenz, the Politburo and the Central Committee resign two days later.

- A military coup attempt begins in the Philippines against the government of Philippine President Corazon C. Aquino. It is crushed by United States intervention ending by December 9.

- December 2 - The Solar Maximother Mission scientific research satellite, launched in 1980, crashes back to earth.

- V. P. Singh takes office as Prime Minister of India.

- In the Republic of China legislative election, the Kuomintang suffers its worst election setback in forty years, winning only 53% of the popular vote.

- The Second Malayan Emergency concludes with a peace agreement. The Malayan Communist Party disbands, and Chin Peng remains in exile in Thailand until his death in 2013.

- December 3 - The entire leadership of the ruling Socialist Unity Party in East Germany, including Egon Krenz, resigns.

- Cold War: Malta Summit – In a meeting off the coast of Malta, U.S. President George H. W. Bush and Soviet leader Mikhail Gorbachev release statements indicating that the Cold War between their nations may be coming to an end.
- December 4 – Prime Minister of Jordan Zaid ibn Shaker resigns and is replaced by Mudar Badran.
- December 6 - The DAS Building bombing occurs in Bogotá, killing 52 people and injuring about 1,000.
- Egon Krenz resigns as Chairman of the State Council of the German Democratic Republic, and is replaced by Manfred Gerlach, the first non-Communist to hold that post.
- École Polytechnique massacre (or Montreal Massacre): Marc Lépine, an anti-feminist gunman, murders fourteen young women at the École Polytechnique de Montréal.
- December 7 - Ladislav Adamec resigns as Prime Minister of Czechoslovakia. He is succeeded by Marián Čalfa on December 10.
- Singing Revolution: The Lithuanian Soviet Socialist Republic becomes the first of the republics of the Soviet Union to abolish the Communist Party's monopoly on power.
- December 9 – The Socialist Unity Party of Germany elects the reformist Gregor Gysi as party leader.
- December 10 - President of Czechoslovakia Gustáv Husák swears in a new cabinet with a non-Communist and then immediately resigns as president.

- Tsakhiagiin Elbegdorj announces the establishment of Mongolia's democratic movement, which peacefully changes the second-oldest Communist country into a democracy.
- December 11 – The International Trans-Antarctica Expedition, a group of six explorers from six nations, reaches the South Pole.
- December 14 – Chile holds its first free election in sixteen years, electing Patricio Aylwin as president.
- December 15 – Drug baron José Gonzalo Rodríguez Gacha is killed by Colombian police.
- December 17 - The Romanian Revolution begins in Timişoara when rioters break into the building housing the District Committee of the Romanian Communist Party and cause extensive damage. Their attempts to set the buildings on fire are foiled by military units.
- Brazil holds the second round of its first free election in 29 years; Fernando Collor de Mello is elected to serve as President from 1990.
- December 19 – Workers in Romanian cities go on strike in protest against the Communist regime.
- December 20 – The United States invasion of Panama ("Operation Just Cause") is launched in an attempt to overthrow Panamanian dictator Manuel Noriega.
- December 21 – Nicolae Ceauşescu addresses an assembly of some 110,000 people outside the Romanian Communist Party headquarters in Bucharest. The crowd begin to protest against

Ceauşescu, and he addresses protesters to calm them down.

- December 22 - After a week of bloody demonstrations, Ion Iliescu takes over as President of Romania, ending the communist dictatorship of Nicolae Ceauşescu, who flees his palace in a helicopter after the palace is invaded by rioters.
- Two tourist coaches collide on the Pacific highway north of Kempsey, Australia, killing 35 people.
- December 23 – Nicolae and Elena Ceauşescu are captured in Târgovişte.
- December 25 - Romanian leader Nicolae Ceauşescu and his wife Elena are executed.
- Bank of Japan governors announce a major interest rate hike, eventually leading to the peak and fall of the bubble economy.
- December 28 – A M 5.6 magnitude earthquake hits Newcastle, New South Wales, Australia, killing 13 people.
- December 29 - Czech writer, philosopher and dissident Václav Havel is elected the first post-Communist President of Czechoslovakia.
- Riots break out after Hong Kong decides to forcibly repatriate Vietnamese refugees.
- Nikkei 225 for Tokyo Stock Exchange hits its all-time intra-day high of 38,957.44 and closing high at 38,915.87.
- Spümcø, the company that produces Ren and Stimpy, is incorporated in California.[22]
- December 31 – Poland's president signs the Balcerowicz Plan, ending the state socialist sys-

tem in Poland in favor of a capitalist system and
Polish involvement in the Warsaw Pact.[23]